Stories of Death by the "Father of the Latin American Short Story"

Written

by

Horacio Quiroga

Published

by

Motmot.org

Translated & Compiled

by

Joaquín de la Sierra

Copyright

Stories of Death by the Father of the Latin American Short Story.
Translation by Joaquin de la Sierra.

© 2022 Motmot.org

Published by Motmot.org

Table of Contents

The Feather Pillow

Their honeymoon was long and chilling. Blond, angelic, and shy, her husband's tough character stopped her girly dreams of a fairy tale marriage. She loved him dearly, sometimes with a slight shiver when coming back down the street at night together, while looking at Jordán's tall stature. He, for his part, loved her deeply, without showing his affections.

For three months, they—having been married in April—lived in special joy. Without a doubt, she would have wanted less seriousness in that rigid sky of love, even more, incautious tenderness, but her husband's impassive countenance always stopped her.

The house they lived in was big and cold. The whiteness of the silent courtyard—marble friezes, columns, and statues—produced an autumn impression of an enchanted palace. Inside, the icy sheen of the stucco, without the slightest scratch on the high walls, affirmed that feeling of unpleasant cold. As they crossed from one room to another, the footsteps echoed throughout the house.

In that strange love nest, Alicia spent the whole fall. However, she had ended up casting a veil over her old dreams. She lived carefree in that hostile house, not wanting to think about anything until her husband arrived.

It was not uncommon for her to lose weight. She had a slight bout of the flu that dragged on insidiously for days that Alicia didn't seem to recover from. Finally, one afternoon she was able to go out into the garden leaning on the arm of her beloved. She looked indifferently from one side to the other. Suddenly Jordán, with deep tenderness, passed his hand over her head, and Alicia immediately broke into sobs, throwing her arms around his neck. She wept for a long time, talking about all her silent terrors, doubling her tears at the slightest attempt at a caress. Then, the sobs slowed down. She remained hidden in his neck for a long time, without moving or saying a word.

That was the last day Alicia was up. The next day she woke up feeling tired and in pain, unable to get on her feet. Jordán's doctor examined her carefully, ordering her absolute rest.

"I don't know," the doctor told Jordán at the front door, his voice still low. "She is very weak, and I can't explain why. There's no vomit, nothing … If she wakes up tomorrow like today, call me right away."

The next day Alicia was still worse. Jordán called the doctor immediately. He discovered that Alicia was suffering from an acute case of anemia, completely unexplainable given her lifestyle. Alicia no longer fainted but was visibly on her way to the grave. All day the bedroom was with the lights on and in complete silence. Hours went by without hearing the slightest noise. Alicia was often asleep. Jordán spent almost every moment in the living room, also with all the lights on. He walked endlessly around the room with tireless obstinacy. The carpet silenced his steps. From time to time, he would go into the bedroom and continue his mute swaying along the bed, glancing at his wife every time he walked in her direction.

Soon, Alicia began to hallucinate. The young woman, with her eyes wide open, was continuously looking at the carpet on both sides of the bed. One night she was suddenly staring at a spot in her living room. After a while she opened her mouth to scream, and her nostrils and lips were covered with sweat.

"Jordán! Jordán!" she cried, stiff with horror, still staring at the carpet.

Jordán ran to the bedroom, and when Alicia saw him appear, she screamed in horror.

"Alicia! It's just me!"

Alicia looked at him confusedly, looked at the carpet, looked at him again, and after a long time of confusion, she calmed down. She smiled and took her husband's hand between hers, trembling.

Among her most stubborn hallucinations, there was an anthropoid, leaning on the carpet on its fingers, its eyes fixed on her.

The doctors returned to no avail. There was a life in front of them that was ending, bleeding day by day, hour by hour, without knowing quite how. At the last consultation, Alicia lay in a stupor while they checked her pulse, passing her inert wrist from one end to the other. They watched her for a long time in silence and then walked to the dining room.

"Pst …" his doctor shrugged discouraged. "It is a serious case … There is little to do …"

"That's all I needed!" Jordán snorted, as he drummed nervously on the table.

Alicia looked worse and worse in her delirium of anemia, aggravated late in the day, but which always remitted in the first hours. During the day her illness did not progress, but every morning she woke up worse. It seemed that only at night her life was slowly lost. When she woke up, she always had the sensation of being slumped in bed with a huge weight on top. From the third day onwards, this horrible feeling never left her. She could barely move her head. She did not want her bed touched or even her pillow fixed. Her twilight terrors advanced in the form of monsters that crawled to her bed and crept towards her.

Then she lost consciousness. The final two days she raved incessantly in a low voice. The lights were still fiercely turned on in the bedroom and living room. In the agonizing silence of the house, nothing was heard except the monotonous delirium coming out of the bed and the muffled sound of the eternal footsteps of Jordán.

Alicia died, finally. The maid, who came in later to undo the bed, already alone, looked at the pillow for a while in surprise.

"Sir!" she called to Jordán in a low voice. "There are stains on the pillow. They look like … blood!"

Jordán approached quickly and took a long, hard look. Indeed, on the cover, on both sides of the spot where Alicia's head stood, there were dark spots.

"They look like bites," the maid murmured after a while of motionless observation.

"Hold it up to the light," Jordán told her.

The maid picked it up, but immediately dropped it and stared at it, livid and trembling. Without knowing why, Jordán felt his hair stand on end.

"What's in there?"

"It's very heavy!" the maid said while trembling.

Jordán picked it up; it was extraordinary in weight. He carried it and left the room. On the dining room table, Jordán cut the pillow's wrap. The upper feathers flew, and the servant girl gave an open-mouthed cry of horror, clasping her clenched hands to the sides. On the bottom, among the feathers, slowly moving its hairy legs, was a monstrous animal, a living, slimy ball. It was so swollen that its mouth was barely visible.

Night after night, since Alicia had fallen into bed, it had stealthily applied its mouth to her temples, sucking her blood. The sting was almost imperceptible. The daily removal of the pillow had undoubtedly impeded its development, but ever since the young woman could no longer move, the suction was constant. In just five nights, it had emptied Alicia.

These parasites of birds, tiny in their usual environment, get to acquire enormous proportions under certain conditions. Human blood seems to be particularly favorable to them, and it is not uncommon to find them on feather pillows.

The Dead Man

The man had just cleared the fifth road of the banana plantation using his machete. He needed to clear two more roads, but as they were abundant with sticks and wild hollyhocks, the task ahead was quite simple. Consequently, the man took a satisfied look at the bushes and crossed the fence to lie down on the grass for a while. But as his body passed the barbed wire, his left foot slipped on a piece of bark detached from the post, just as the machete slipped from his hand. As he fell, the man had the extremely distant impression of not seeing the machete fall flat on the ground.

He was already lying on the grass, lying on his right side, just as he wanted. His mouth, which had just opened to its full extent, had just closed as well. He was lying down comfortably, as he would have liked to be, his knees bent and his left hand on his chest. Except that behind his forearm, and immediately below his belt, the fist and half of the machete blade emerged from his shirt, but the rest of it was not visible.

The man tried to shake his head in vain. He cast a sideways glance at the hilt of the machete, still damp from the sweat on his hand. He appreciated the extension and trajectory of the machete inside his belly and acquired the cold, mathematical and inexhaustible assurance that he had just reached the end of his existence.

Death: In the course of life, it's common to think that one day, after years, months, weeks, and days, we will arrive in our turn at the threshold of death. It is the fatal law, accepted and foreseen; So much so that we tend to let imagination take pleasure of that moment, supreme among all, when we take our last breath. But between the present moment and that final expiration, what dreams, upheavals, hopes, and dramas we boast in our lives! What does this vigorous existence still have in store for us before our elimination from the human scene! This is the consolation, the pleasure, and the reason for our mortuary ramblings: Death is so far away and so unforeseen that we must still live! Still...?

Not two seconds have passed: the sun is precisely at the same height; The shadows haven't advanced a millimeter. Abruptly; the ramblings have just dissipated for the man: he is dying. Dead. He can be considered dead in his comfortable posture. But the man opens his eyes and looks. How much time has passed? What cataclysm has survived in the world? What upheaval of nature betrays the horrible event?

He is going to die. Coldly, fatally and inescapably, he is going to die.

The man resists—the horror of death is so unexpected—And thinks: This is just a nightmare! And he looks ahead: isn't that the banana plantation? Does he not come every morning to clean it? Who knows it as he does? He sees the banana plantation perfectly, very bright, and the broad bare leaves under the sun. There they are, very close, frayed by the wind. But now they are not moving. Through the bananas, the man sees the red roof of his house. To the left, he glimpsed at the mountain. He can't see more, but he knows very well that behind him is the road to the new port and that in the direction of his head, down there, lies at the bottom of the valley the Paraná river asleep like a lake. Everything else is exactly as always; the fiery sun, the vibrant and lonely air, the immobile bananas, the very thick and tall wire fence.

Dead! But is it possible? Isn't this one of the many days that he has left home at dawn with a machete in hand? Isn't the horse right there, four meters from him, his Malacara, sniffing the barbed wire? Yes, of course! Someone whistles. He cannot see because his back is to the road, but he feels the horse's footsteps drawing nearer. It is the boy that passes through every morning to the new port at eleven-thirty, always whistling. From the post that almost reaches his boots to the mountain fence that separates the banana plantation from the road, there's a distance of fifteen meters. He knows it perfectly well because he measured the distance when he built the fence.

What's the matter, then? Is it not a natural noon of the many in Misiones, on its mountain, in its pasture, in the sparse banana plantation? Definitely! Short grass, ant cones, silence, hot sun. Nothing, absolutely nothing has changed. Only he is different. For two minutes, his person, his living personality, has nothing to do with either the paddock, which he built himself, or the banana plantation, the works of his own hands. Nor with his family. His life has been roughly torn off, naturally, by the result of a machete to the belly.

The man, very tired and lying on the grass on his right side, is always reluctant to admit a phenomenon of this transcendence, given the ordinary and monotonous aspect of everything he sees. He knows the time well: eleven-thirty. The boy has just crossed the bridge.

But it is not possible that he slipped ...! The handle of his machete (he will soon have to exchange it for another as it's already very worn out) was perfectly pressed between his left hand and the barbed wire. After ten years in the forest, he knows very well how to handle a bush machete. He is just exhausted from work that morning and rests for a while as usual. But the grass that now enters through the corner of his mouth, he planted it himself in loaves of earth a meter away from each other! and that's the Malacara, snorting cautiously at the barbs of the wire! He sees everything perfectly; He knows that the Malacara doesn't dare to turn the corner of the fence because he is lying almost at the foot of the post. The sun is beating down, and the calm is very significant because not a fringe of the bananas moves. Every day he has seen the same things.

He was exhausted, resting alone. It must have been several minutes since the incident. And at a quarter to twelve, from up there, from the chalet with the red roof, his wife and his two sons will come off to the banana plantation to look for him for lunch. Before the others, he always hears the voice of his youngest boy who wants to let go of the hand of his mother: "¡Father! Father!"

He hears the voice of his son. What a nightmare! But it is one of many days, trivial as all, of course! Excessive light and yellowish shadows make the Malacara sweat before the dying man.

Very tired, but nothing more. How many times, at noon like now, has he crossed that pasture, returning home, which was a grazing field when he arrived so many years ago. He would then return, very tired too, slowly, with his machete hanging from his left hand. He can still walk away with his mind if he wants to; He can, if he wants, to leave his body for a moment and see from the roof he built the usual trivial landscape: the volcanic gravel with rigid grass; the banana plantation and its red sand. And further still to see the pasture, work alone of his hands. And at the foot of a chipped post, lying on his right side and his legs folded up, exactly like every day, he can see himself, as a small sunny bundle on the grass — resting, because he is exhausted.

But the horse, streaked with sweat and motionless with caution before the corner of the fence, also sees the man on the ground and does not dare to cross the banana plantation. Ahead of the voices that are already close by —"Papa!" —the horse turns around: and finally reassured, decided to pass between the post and the lying man who was already dead.

The Spectre

Every night at the Grand Splendid in Santa Fe, Enid and I go to movie premieres. Neither storms nor frosty nights have prevented us from entering, at ten o'clock, into the warm gloom of the theater. From one balcony or another, we follow the stories of the film with such silence and interest that others might reprimand us for it if the circumstances in which we act were different.

From one balcony or another, it doesn't matter; because its location is indifferent to us. And even if the theater is sold out some night, because the movie The Splendid is in full swing, we settle down, mute and always attentive to the performance in any already occupied balcony. We don't get in the way, I think; Or, at least, in a sensible way. From the back of the balcony, or between the girl on the windowsill and the boyfriend clinging to the back of her neck, Enid and I, apart from the world around us, are all eyes towards the screen. And if indeed someone, with chills of concern whose origin he cannot understand, sometimes turns his head to see what he cannot, or feels an icy breath that cannot be explained in the warm atmosphere, our presence of intruders is never noticed; for it is necessary to warn now that Enid and I are dead.

Of all the women I met in the living world, none affected me as Enid. The impression was so strong that the image and the very memory of all the women were erased. In my soul, it was night, where a single imperishable star rose: Enid. The mere possibility of her eyes gazing at me without indifference made my heart abruptly stop. And at the thought that she could ever be mine, my jaw twitched. Enid!

When we lived in the world, she had the most divine beauty that the movie industry has launched and exposed to the fixed gaze of men. Above all, her eyes were unique; and never did a velvet had a frame of lashes like Enid's eyes; blue, damp, and calm, like the happiness that sobbed in her.

Misfortune put me before her when she was already married.

I will not hide any names. Everyone remembers Duncan Wyoming, the extraordinary actor. He, beginning his career at the same time as William Hart, had, like him and alongside him, the same profound virtues of virile acting. Hart has given the movies everything we could hope for from him, and he is a falling star. On the other hand, of Wyoming, we don't know what we might have seen, when just at the beginning of his short and fantastic career, he created—in contrast to the sentimental hero of today—the rude, rough, ugly, kind of man.

Hart kept acting, and we have already seen him repeatedly.

According to company reports, Wyoming was snatched from us in his prime age, at a time when two extraordinary tapes were ending: *El Paramo* and *Beyond What You See*.

But the charm—the absorption of all the feelings of a man — that Enid wielded on me had but one bitterness: Wyoming, who was her husband, was also my best friend.

We had not seen Duncan for two years; he was busy with his works, and I was busy with literature. When I found him again in Hollywood, he was already married.

"Here is my wife," he said, throwing her into my arms.

He said to her: "Hold him tight, like a brother, because you won't have a friend like Grant. And kiss him if you want."

She did not kiss me, but when her hair caressed my neck, I felt a chill through all my nerves, making it clear that I could never be like a brother to that woman.

We lived in Canada for two months together, and it is not difficult to understand my state of mind regarding Enid. But not in a word, not in a movement, not in a gesture did I reveal my intentions to Wyoming. Only she read in my gaze, no matter how calm, how deeply I wanted her.

Love and desire. The one and the other were twins in me, sharp and mixed because if I desired her with all the might of my disembodied soul, I adored her with all the torrent of my substantial blood.

Duncan didn't see it. How could he?

At the beginning of winter, we returned to Hollywood and Wyoming then fell sick with the flu, which eventually cost him his life. He left his widow wealthy and childless. But he was not calm because of the loneliness of his wife.

"It's not the economic situation," he told me, "but moral distress. And in this hell of the movie industry, it is worse."

At the moment of death, lowering his wife and me to the pillow, and with pain in his voice, he said:

"Trust Grant, Enid ... As long as you have him, fear nothing. And you, old friend, watch over her. Be her brother. Now I can go to the other side in peace."

For some time, nothing changed in the pain Enid and I experienced. Seven days later, we returned to Canada, to the same summer hut that a month earlier had seen the three of us dine in front of the fireplace. As then, Enid now gazed at the fire, hugged by the icy serene, while I stood, contemplating her. And Duncan was not with us anymore.

I must say it: in the death of Wyoming, I saw nothing but the liberation of the terrible eagle caged in the hearts of men, which is the desire of a woman that cannot be touched. I had been Wyoming's best friend, and while he lived, the eagle did not want his blood; He fed—I fed it—on my own. But something more consistent than a shadow had arisen between him and me. His wife was, while he lived—and would have been forever—intangible to me. But he had died. Wyoming could not demand the sacrifice of life in which he had just failed. And Enid was my life, my future, my encouragement, and my desire to live, which no one, not Duncan—my close friend, but dead—could deny me.

"Watch over her..." Those words resounded in my mind. Yes, I'll watch over her by giving her what he had taken from her when he lost his turn: the worship of a whole life devoted to her!

For two months, by her side day and night, I watched over her like a brother. But on the third, I fell at her feet.

Enid stared at me immobile, and surely the last moments of Wyoming rose to her memory because she rejected me violently. But I did not remove my head from her skirt.

"I love you, Enid," I told her. "Without you, I die."

"You, Guillermo!" She murmured. "It is horrible to hear you say this!"

"Anything you want." I replied. "But I love you immensely."

"Shut up, shut up!"

"And I have always loved you ... You know ..."

"No, no, I do not know!"

"Yes, you know."

Enid always pushed me aside, and I resisted with my head between her knees.

"Tell me you knew ..."

"No shut up! We are desecrating the memory of Wyoming ..."

"Tell me you knew ..."

"Guillermo!"

"Just tell me that you knew that I have always loved you ..."

Her arms gave up wearily, and I raised my head. I met her eyes instantly before Enid yielded to cry on her knees.

I left her alone, and when an hour later I came back in, white with snow, no one would have suspected, seeing our simulated and calm affection of every day, that we had just stretched, until we made them bleed, the strings of our hearts.

Because in the alliance of Enid and Wyoming, there had never been love. There was always a blaze of folly, misguidance, injustice—the flame of passion that burns a man's entire morale and burns a woman in long sobs of fire. Enid had loved her husband, nothing more, and she had wanted him, nothing more.

Death, then, left a gap that I had to fill with the affection of a brother. As a brother to her, Enid, was my only source of happiness in the entire world!

Three days after the scene I have just related, we returned to Hollywood. And a month later, precisely the same situation was repeating itself: me again at Enid's feet with my head on her knees, and she wanting to avoid it.

"I love you more every day, Enid ..."

"Guillermo!"

"Tell me that one day you will love me."

"No!"

"Just tell me that you are convinced of how much I love you."

"No!"

"Say it!"

"Leave me alone! Can't you see that you are making me suffer horribly?"

And when she felt me trembling mutely on the altar of her knees, she abruptly raised my face between her hands:

"But let me tell you! Let me! Don't you see that I also love you with all my soul and that we are committing a crime?"

Just four months, one hundred and twenty days barely elapsed since the death of the man she loved, of the friend who had interposed me like a protective veil between his wife and new love.

So deep and penetrating was our love that even today, I wonder with astonishment what absurd purpose our lives could have had if they had not found us under the arms of Wyoming.

One night—we were in New York—I found out that *El Páramo* was finally showing, one of the two films I have talked about and whose release was eagerly awaited. I also had the keenest interest in seeing her and proceeded to ask Enid to accompany me.

We looked at each other for a long time, an eternity of silence, during which the memory galloped backward between falling snow and dying faces. But Enid's gaze was life itself, between the damp velvet of her eyes and mine, she controlled the convulsive bliss of adoring each other and nothing more.

We went to the cinema, and from the reddish gloom of the balcony, we saw Duncan Wyoming appear, huge and with a face whiter than when he died. I felt Enid's arm tremble under my hand.

"Duncan!"

The same usual confident smile from always was on his lips. It was his energetic figure gliding along with the screen. And twenty meters from him, was his own woman who was under the fingers of his close friend.

While the room was dark, neither Enid nor I spoke a word or stopped looking at each other for a moment. Long tears were rolling down her cheeks, and she was smiling at me. I was smiling without trying to hide her tears from me.

"Yes, I understand, my love," I murmured. "I understand, but let us not give up. Yes? We will forget."

Enid, always smiling at me, gathered herself mutely to my neck.

The next night we returned. Should we forget? The actor's presence, vibrant in the beam of light that transported him to the pulsating screen of life; his unconsciousness of the situation; his trust in the woman and his friend; this was precisely what we had to get used to.

Over and over again, always attentive to the characters, we witnessed the growing success of *El Páramo*.

Wyoming's performance was outstanding, unfolding in a brute-energy drama: a small part in Canada's forests and the rest in New York itself. The central situation was when Wyoming, wounded in a fight with a man, abruptly has the revelation of his wife's love for this man, whom he had just killed for reasons other than their love. Wyoming had just tied a scarf to her forehead. And lying on the couch, still panting with fatigue, he witnessed the despair of his wife over the corpse of her lover.

Seldom has the revelation of collapse, desolation, and hatred come to the human face with more violent clarity than in Wyoming's eyes. The film's direction had squeezed that prodigy of expression to torture, and the scene was sustained for an infinite number of seconds when only one second was enough to show the red-white crisis of a heart in that state.

Enid and I, together and motionless in the dark, admired like nobody else the dead friend, whose eyelashes almost touched us when Wyoming came from the bottom to fill the screen himself. And as he walked away back to the scene of the set, the entire room seemed to respond accordingly. And Enid and I, slightly dizzy, still felt the rub of Duncan's hair that had come to touch us.

Why did we keep going to the cinema? What deviation of our consciences led us there night after night to soak our pure love in blood? What omen was dragging us like sleepwalkers before a hallucinatory accusation that was not directed at us since Wyoming's eyes were turned the other way?

Where were they looking? I don't know where, maybe to another balcony on our left. But one night, I noticed, I felt it in the roots of the hair, that the eyes were turning towards us. Enid must have seen it too, because I felt the deep shake of her shoulders under my hand.

There are natural laws, physical principles that teach us how cold magic is that of photographic specters dancing on the screen, mimicking even in the most intimate details a lost life. That black and white hallucination is only the frozen persistence of an instant, the immutable relief of a vital second. It would be easier for us to see by our side a dead man who leaves the grave to accompany us than to perceive the slightest change in the livid face of a film.

Perfectly. But despite the laws and principles, Wyoming was watching us. If for the living room, *El Páramo* was a fictional movie, and Wyoming lived only by an irony of light; If it was nothing more than an electric foil front without sides or bottom, for us—Wyoming, Enid and I—the filmed scene lived flagrantly, but not on the screen, but in a balcony, where our guiltless love was transformed into monstrous infidelity in the face of the husband alive.

Was Duncan's visible anger only the pretended hatred on that scene of *El Paramo*?

Of course not! There was the brutal revelation; the tender wife and the close friend in the showroom, laughing, heads together, at the trust placed in them.

But we quickly stopped laughing, because night by night, movie after movie, the gaze was turning more and more towards us.

"His gaze is coming closer and closer!" I said to myself.

"Tomorrow he'll look straight at us." Enid thought.

As the cinema burned with light, the real world of physical laws took hold of us, and we breathed deeply.

But in the abrupt cessation of light, which we felt painfully on our nerves like a blow, the spectral drama caught us again.

A thousand leagues from New York, boxed under the ground, Duncan Wyoming lay without eyes. But his surprise at Enid's frenzied forgetfulness, his anger, and his revenge were alive there, igniting Wyoming's chemical trail, moving into his living eyes, which had finally just fixed on ours.

Enid gasped and hugged desperately to me.

"Guillermo!"

"Quiet, please."

"It is that now he has just taken one leg off the couch!"

I felt the skin on my back crawl, and I looked:

With extreme slowness and eyes fixed on us, Wyoming rose from the divan. Enid and I saw him rise, advance towards us from the back of the scene, come to the monstrous foreground. A dazzling glare blinded us while Enid let out a cry.

The tape had just burned.

But in the lighted room, heads were all turned towards us. Some sat up to see what was happening.

"The lady is ill; she looks like a dead woman", said someone in the audience.

"He seems far worse," added another.

What else? Nothing, but the next day Enid and I did not see each other. Only, days after, when we first looked at each other at night to go to the cinema, Enid already had the darkness of the afterlife in her deep pupils, and I had a revolver in my pocket.

I do not know if anyone in the room recognized us as the sick couple from the night before. The lights went out, went on, and went out again, without a single abnormal idea being able to settle in Guillermo Grant's brain and without clenching fingers leaving the trigger for a moment.

No one noticed anything unusual on the screen the previous night, and Wyoming was still panting on the couch. But Enid—Enid in my arms—had her face turned to the light, ready to scream when Wyoming finally got up.

I saw him get ahead, stand up, reach the very edge of the screen without taking his gaze from mine. I saw him detach itself, come towards us in the beam of light; He came in the air over the heads of the audience, rising, coming up to us with his head bandaged. I saw him extend the claws of his fingers, just as Enid gave a horrible scream, the kind in which a vocal cord may rupture.

I can't tell what happened in the first instant. But after the first moments of confusion and smoke, I found myself with my body hanging off the balcony, dead.

From the moment Wyoming was sitting on the couch, I aimed the barrel of my revolver at his head. I remember it clearly. And it was I who had taken the bullet to the temple.

I am entirely sure I wanted to aim the gun at Duncan. Only, believing I was aiming at the murderer, I was actually aiming at myself. It was a mistake, a simple mistake, nothing more, but it cost me my life.

Three days later, Enid was in turn evicted from the world. And here our idyll ends.

But it is not over yet. A shot and a specter are not enough to vanish a love like ours. Beyond death, life, and their grudges, Enid and I have found each other. Invisible within the living world, Enid and I are always together, waiting for the announcement of another film premiere.

We have traveled the world. Everything can be expected unless the slightest incident in a film goes unnoticed in our eyes. We have not seen *El Paramo* again. Wyoming's performance in it can no longer bring us surprises, other than those that we so painfully paid for.

Now our hope is on *Beyond What Is Seen*. For seven years, the film company has announced its premiere, and for seven years, Enid and I have waited. Duncan is its protagonist, but we will no longer be on the balcony, at least in our usual conditions. In the present circumstances, Duncan may make a mistake that allows us to re-enter the visible world in the same way that we, seven years ago, allowed him to animate the icy sheet of his film.

Enid and I now occupy, in the invisible fog of the disembodied, the privileged lurking spot that was Wyoming's entire force in the previous drama. If they persist, if he makes a mistake in seeing us and makes the slightest movement out of the grave, we will take advantage. The curtain that separates life from death has not been drawn solely in the favor of the living, and the war is ongoing. Between the Nothingness that has dissolved what Wyoming was and the electric resurrection, there remains a space. With the most slight movement the actor makes, as soon as he detaches himself from the screen, Enid and I will slide as if through a fissure in the dark corridor. But we will not follow the road to Wyoming's grave; We will return to life, and it is the warm world from which we are expelled, the tangible and vibrant love of every human sense, that awaits Enid and me then.

In a month or a year, the movie will arrive. We are only concerned about the possibility that *Beyond What Is Seen* will be released under another name, as is customary in this city. Therefore, we never miss a premiere. Night after night we enter the cinema at ten o'clock, where we settle in a balcony, either empty or already occupied, it does not matter.

The Beyond

"I was desperate," said the voice. "My parents were adamantly opposed to me having love affairs with him, and they had become very cruel to me. The last few days, they did not even let him show up at the door. Before, I saw him for just an instant standing on the corner, waiting for me since the morning. Afterward, not even that!"

I told my mother the week before:

"But what do you and Papa think of him? Why do you torture me like that? Do you have anything to say about him? Why have you objected, as if he were unworthy to set foot in this house, or even for him to visit me?"

Mom made me leave. Dad, who was coming in at that moment, stopped me by the arm, and when Mom found out what I had said, she pushed me out by the shoulder, throwing me from behind:

"Your mother is wrong; what she has meant is that she and I—do you hear it right? —we'd rather see you dead than in the arms of that man. And not a word more about this."

"Very well," I replied, turning, paler than the tablecloth itself, "I will never speak to you about him again."

And I entered my room slowly, deeply amazed to feel what I felt because, at that moment, I had decided to die.

Die! To finally let go of that everyday hell, knowing that he was two steps away, waiting to see me and suffering more than me! All because my father would never consent to my marriage with Luis. What didn't he approve? I still wonder. That he was poor? We were as much as he was.

Oh! I knew my father's stubbornness, as did my mother.

"Killed a thousand times," he said, "rather than giving her to that man."

But for him, my father, what did he give me instead, if it wasn't the misfortune of loving with all my being knowing myself loved and condemned not even to see him at the door for a moment?

Dying was preferable, yes, dying together.

I knew that he could kill himself, but I, who alone did not find the strength to fulfill my destiny, felt that once at his side, I would prefer a thousand times death together to the despair of never seeing him again.

I wrote him a letter, willing to do anything. A week later, we were in the agreed place, and we were occupying a room in the same hotel.

I cannot say I was proud of what I was going to do, nor was I happy to die. It was something more fatal, more frantic, more without remission, as if from the depths of the past my grandparents, my great-grandparents, my childhood itself, my first communion, my dreams as if all this had no other purpose than to drive me to suicide.

We did not feel happy, I repeat, to die. We abandoned life because it had already left us by preventing us from being with each other. In the first, pure, and last hug that we gave each other on the bed, dressed and in shoes as when we arrived, I understood, marked with happiness in his arms, how great my joy would have been if I had become his girlfriend, his wife.

At once, we drank the poison. In the concise space of time between receiving the glass from his hand and bringing it to my mouth, those same forces of my parents that rushed me to death suddenly appeared on the edge of my destiny to contain me. Too late! Suddenly, all the noises from the street, from the city itself, ceased; they fell back vertiginously before me, leaving an enormous place in its hollow as if up to that moment the area had been filled with a thousand familiar cries.

I remained still for two seconds, with my eyes open. And suddenly, I seized him convulsively, free at last from my dreadful loneliness.

Yes, I was with him; and we were going to die in an instant!

The poison was atrocious, and Luis first began the step that led us together to the grave.

"Forgive me," he said, still pressing my head against his neck. "I love you so much that I am taking you with me."

"And I love you," I replied, "and I die with you."

I could not speak anymore. But what sound of footsteps, what voices came from the corridor to indulge our agony? What frantic knocks echoed at the door itself?

"They followed me and came to separate us." I murmured still. "But I am all yours."

In the end, I realized that I had spoken those words in my mind because, at that moment, I was losing consciousness.

* * *

When I came to my senses, I had the impression that I would fall if I did not look for a place to support myself. I felt light and so rested that even the sweetness of opening my eyes was sensitive to me. I was standing in the same hotel room, leaning almost against the far wall. And there, next to the bed, was my desperate mother.

So had they saved me? I turned my eyes to all sides, and next to the nightstand, standing like me, I saw Luis, who had just distinguished me in turn and came smiling. We went straight to each other, despite the significant number of people around the bed, and we said nothing, for our eyes expressed all the happiness of being together.

Seeing him, diaphanous and visible through everything and everyone, I had just realized that I was like him: dead.

We had died; despite my fear of being saved when I lost consciousness, we had lost our lives, fortunately. And there, in bed, my desperate mother was screaming while the hotel waiter removed my arms from the head of my beloved.

Far in the background, with joined hands, Luis and I saw everything in a clear perspective, cold and without passion. Three steps away, without a doubt, we were, killed by suicide, surrounded by the desolation of my relatives, the owner of the hotel, and the swaying of the police. What did we care about that?

"My love!" Luis said to me. "At what little price have we bought our eternal happiness!"

"And I," I replied, "will always love you as I loved you before. And we will not part anymore, right?"

"Oh no! ... We've already tried it."

"And are you going to visit me every night?"

While we were exchanging our promises, we heard my mother's violent screams, which reached us with an inert sound and no echo as if they could not penetrate the environment that surrounded Mom by more than a meter.

We looked back inside the room. They were carrying our corpses at last, and it must have been a long time since we died, for we could see that both Luis and I already had rigid joints and very stiff fingers.

Our bodies lay there. Had there been something of our life, our tenderness, in those two weighty bodies that came down the stairs, threatening to roll everyone with them?

Dead! How absurd! What had lived in us, more potent than life itself, continued to live with all the hopes of eternal love. Before, I had not even been able to peek out the door to see him; now, I would regularly talk to him as he would come home as my boyfriend.

"When are you going to visit me?" I asked.

"Tomorrow," he said. "Let us rest today."

"Why tomorrow?" I asked, anguished. "Isn't it the same today? Come tonight, Luis! I want to be alone with you in the living room!"

"Me too! At nine, then?"

"Yes. See you later, my love..."

And we parted ways. I returned home slowly, happy, and relieved as if I was returning from the first love date of my life.

* * *

At nine o'clock I ran to the front door and received my boyfriend myself. He is home, visiting!

"Do you know that the room is full of people?"—I asked—"But they won't bother us."

"Of course not ... Is your corpse there?"

"Yes."

"Very disfigured?"

"Not much at all. Come, let's see!"

We entered the room. Despite the temples' lividness and the very tight nostrils, my face was almost the same as Luis expected to see.

"You look very similar," he said.

"Right?" I replied, happy. And we immediately forgot everything, lulling each other.

At times, however, we suspended our conversation and watched the crowd go in and out. In one of those moments, I caught the attention of Luis.

"Look!"—I said—"What do you think will happen?"

Indeed, the agitation of the people, very much alive for a few minutes before, was accentuated by the entry into the room of a new coffin. New people, not yet seen there, accompanied it.

"It's me," Luis said with slight surprise. "My sisters come too".

"Look, Luis!" I observed. "They put our corpses in the exact position as we were when we died."

"As we should always be," he added. And fixing his eyes for a long time on the face excavated with the pain of his sisters:

"Poor girls …" he murmured with grave tenderness. I got close to him, won by the belated homage, but bloody atonement, overcoming who knows what difficulties my parents made by burying us together.

"They are burying us. What madness!" Lovers who have committed suicide on a hotel bed, pure in body and soul, live forever. Nothing linked us to those two cold and rigid bodies, now nameless, in which life had been broken with pain. And despite everything, however, they had been too dear to us in another existence for us not to cast a long look full of memories on those two cadaverous ghosts of love.

"Our corpses too," said my beloved, "will be together forever."

"But I'm with you," I murmured, raising my eyes to him happily. And we forgot everything again.

* * *

"For three months," the voice continued, "I lived in full bliss. My boyfriend visits me twice a week. He would arrive at nine o'clock, without a single night having been delayed a single second, and without a single time, I had failed to meet him at the door. My boyfriend did not always observe the same punctuality to retire. Eleven-thirty, even twelve, without him deciding to let go of my hands, without me being able to tear my gaze from his. He was leaving at last, and I was happily surrendered, pacing around the room with my face resting on the palm of my hand."

During the day, I shortened the hours by thinking about him. I went back and forth from room to room, watching my family's movement without any interest. However, more than once I stopped at the dining room door to contemplate the gloomy pain of my mother, who sometimes broke into desperate sobs at the empty place of the table where her youngest daughter used to sit down.

I lived—survived—by love and for love. Outside of him, of my loved one, of the presence of the memory of him, everything acted for me in a world apart. And even when I was close to my family, an invisible and transparent abyss opened between them and me, separating us a thousand leagues.

Luis and I also went out at night, as the official couple that we were. There is no walk that we have not traveled together, nor twilight in which we have not slipped our idyll. When there was a full moon and the temperature was cool at night, we liked to extend our walks to the city's outskirts, where we felt freer, purer, and more loving.

One of those nights, as our footsteps had brought us to the view of the cemetery, we were curious to see where our corpses were lying underground. We entered the vast enclosure and stopped before a dark patch of land, where a marble tombstone gleamed. It bore our only two names, and underneath the date of our death, nothing more.

"As I remember us," Luis observed, "it couldn't be shorter. Still," he added after a pause, "it contains more tears and regrets than many long epitaphs."

After he said that, we were silent again.

Perhaps in that place and at that hour, we would have given the impression of being foolish to those who observed us. But my boyfriend and I knew well that what was fatuous and without redemption were those two specters of a double suicide locked up at our feet, and reality, life purified of errors, rose pure and sublimated in us like two flames of the same love.

We left there, happy and without memories, to walk along the white road, our happiness without limits.

Isolated from the world, with no other end or other thought than to see each other in order to see each other again, our love ascended. We both began to feel a lovely melancholy when we were together and extreme sadness when we were apart. I forgot to say that my boyfriend visited me every night then, but we spent almost all the time without speaking as if our phrases of affection had no value to express what we felt. Each time he retired later, when everyone was asleep at home, and each time when he left, we shortened our farewell.

We went out and returned speechless because I knew well that what he could say to me did not respond to his thoughts, and he was sure that I would answer him anything, to avoid looking at him.

One night when our uneasiness had reached an unbearable limit, Luis said goodbye to me later than usual. And as he extended his hands to me, and I gave him my frozen ones, I read in his eyes, with intolerable transparency, what was happening to us. I turned as pale as death itself, and as his hands did not let go of mine:

"Luis!" I murmured in horror, feeling that my disembodied life was desperately seeking support, as in any other circumstance. He understood our situation's horribleness because releasing my hands with a courage that I now appreciate; his eyes regained unmistakable tenderness.

"See you tomorrow, my love," he said, smiling.

"See you tomorrow, love," I murmured, paling even more as I said this.

Because in that instant, I had just realized that I would never be able to utter these words again.

Luis returned the next night; we went out together, we talked, we talked like we never had before, and like we did on previous nights. All in vain: we could no longer look at each other. We said goodbye briefly, without touching each other.

Last night my boyfriend fell suddenly before me and put his head on my knees.

"My love," he murmured.

"Shut up!"—I said.

"My love," he began.

"Luis! Shut up!" I replied, terrified. "If you repeat that…"

His head rose, and our ghostly eyes—this is horrible to say! —Met for the first time in many days.

"What?" Luis asked. "What if I say it?"

"You know what happens," I replied.

"Tell me!"

"You know! I'm dying!"

For fifteen seconds, our gazes were linked with tremendous fixation. In that time, running as if by the thread of destiny, endless love stories, truncated, resumed, broken, revived, defeated, and finally sunk in the dread of the impossible.

"I'm dying …" I began to murmur, responding to his gaze. He understood it too, for sinking his forehead back into my knees, he raised his voice for a long time.

'We have but one thing to do …" he said.

"I think so," I said.

"You understand me?" Luis insisted.

"Yes, I understand you," I replied, placing my hands on his head so that he would let me sit up. And without looking back, we headed to the cemetery.

Ah! You cannot play at love, at a couple, when the mouth to kiss was burned in suicide! One does not play at life, at sobbing passion, when from the bottom of a coffin two corpses ask us to account for our imitation and our falsehood! Love! An unpronounceable word when used after taking a cup of cyanide to enjoy dying!

"That kiss cost us our lives," the voice concludes, "and we know it."

When you have died once of love, you must die again. A while ago, when Luis picked up himself, I would have given up my soul to be kissed. In an instant, he will kiss me, and what in us was sublime and unsustainable fictional fog will descend, vanish at the critical and always faithful contact of our mortal remains.

I do not know what awaits us beyond. But if our love was one day capable of rising over our poisoned bodies and managed to live for three months in the hallucination of an idyll, perhaps a primitive and essential urn of that love has resisted the contingencies that await us.

Standing on the tombstone, Luis and I look at each other long and freely. His arms encircle my waist, his mouth seeks my mouth, and I give him a deep kiss with such passion that I vanish.

The Slaughtered Hen

All day, sitting out on the patio, on a bench were the four idiotic sons of the Mazzini-Ferraz couple. Their tongues were between their lips, their eyes were stupid, and they turned their heads with their mouths open.

The courtyard was closed to the west by a brick fence. The bench was parallel to it, five meters away, and there they sat motionless, their eyes fixed on the bricks. As the sun was setting behind the fence, when it descended, the idiots smiled for the first time that day. The blinding light caught their attention at first, little by little their eyes brightened; they laughed uproariously at last, congested by the same eager hilarity, gazing at the sun with bestial joy, as if it were food.

Other times, they could be found lined up on the bench, they hummed for hours, imitating the electric tram. Loud noises also shook their inertia, and they would then run, biting their tongues, around the courtyard. But most of the time they were dull in a gloomy lethargy of idiocy, and they sat all day on their bench, their legs dangling and still, their pants soaking in thick saliva.

The oldest was twelve and the youngest eight. In all their dirty and disheveled appearance, you could see the absolute lack of even the smallest amount of motherly care.

Those four idiots, however, had once been the charm of their parents. Three months after they were married, Mazzini and Berta directed their close love as husband and wife, and wife and husband, towards a much more vital future: a child. What greater happiness for two lovers than that of an honest consecration of their affection, already freed from the vile selfishness of a mutual love without end?

That was how Mazzini and Berta felt, and when their son arrived, fourteen months after their marriage, they believed their happiness had been fulfilled. The creature grew beautiful and radiant, until he was a year and a half. But in the twentieth month he seized one night with terrible convulsions, and the next morning he no longer knew his parents. The doctor examined him with professional care and attention, looking for the root cause of his affliction in his parents' disease history.

After a few days his paralyzed extremities regained movement; but his intelligence, his soul, even his instinct, were completely gone; he had remained deeply idiotic, slimy, hanging, dead forever on his mother's knees.

"Son, my dear son!" She was sobbing, over that dreadful ruin of her first-born.

The father, devastated, accompanied the doctor outside.

"I can say this to you: I think it's a lost cause. He can improve, educate himself in whatever his idiocy allows, but no further."

"Yes, Yes!" Mazzini agreed. "But tell me: Do you think his disease was inherited?"

"As for the paternal inheritance, I already told you what I believed when I saw your son. Regarding the mother, there is a lung that does not look well. I don't see anything else. I will examine him more carefully."

Soul-shattered with remorse, Mazzini redoubled his love for his son, the little idiot who paid for his grandfather's excesses. He also had to console, relentlessly support Berta, deeply wounded by that failure of her young motherhood.

Naturally, the couple put all their love in the hope of another child. This one was born, and his health and clarity of laughter rekindled the extinct future. But at eighteen months the convulsions of the first-born were repeated, and the next day the second son woke up as an idiot.

This time the parents fell into deep despair. Their blood and their love were cursed! Their love, above all! All his twenty-eight years and all her twenty-two, and all their passionate tenderness could not create an atom of normal life. They no longer asked for more beauty and intelligence as in the first-born.

From the new disaster sprang new flames of aching love, a mad longing to redeem once and for all the sanctity of their tenderness. Twins ensued shortly afterwards, and the process of the two older ones was repeated.

But above their immense bitterness, Mazzini and Berta had great compassion for their four children.

They didn't know how to swallow, change places, or even sit. They finally learned to walk, but they crashed into everything, because they were unaware of the obstacles. When they were washed, they yelled until their faces turned red. They were amused only by eating, or when they saw bright colors or heard thunder. They laughed then, spouting tongues and rivers of slime, radiant with bestial frenzy. They had a certain imitative faculty; but nothing else.

The birth of the twins seemed to have concluded that terrible lineage. But after three years they once again longed for another child, hoping that the long time that had passed would have appeased doom.

Their hopes were not met. And in that burning longing that was exasperated by reason of their fruitlessness, they soured. Up to that moment each one had taken the part that corresponded to the misery of their children; but the hopelessness of redemption in the face of the four beasts that had been born from them cast out that urgent need to blame others, which is the specific patrimony of inferior hearts.

They started with the change of pronoun: your children. And as besides the insult there was the insidiousness, the atmosphere was charged.

"It seems to me"—Mazzini said to her one night, who had just come in and was washing her hands—"that you could wash the boys more often."

Berta continued reading as if she had not heard him.

"It is the first time," she replied after a while "that I see you worry about the state of your children."

Mazzini turned his face to her a little with a forced smile:

"Of OUR children."

"Well, of our children. You like it like that?" She raised her eyes.

This time Mazzini made it clear:

"I don't think you're going to say it's my fault, right?"

"Oh no!" Berta smiled at herself, very pale, "but neither was mine. Not my fault!" She murmured.

"What is not your fault?"

"That if someone is to blame, it's not me, get it right! This is what I wanted to tell you."

Her husband looked at her for a moment, with a brutal desire to insult her.

"Let's stop!" He mouthed, finally wiping his hands.

"As you like; but if you want to say …"

"Berta!"

"Have it your way!"

This was the first crash and was succeeded by others. But in the inevitable reconciliations, their souls joined in madness for another child.

Thus, a girl was born. They lived two years in anguish with the flower of their soul, always waiting for another disaster. Nothing happened, however, and the parents put all their complacency on her, that the little girl took to the most extreme limits of pampering and bad upbringing.

Even though Berta always took care of her children, when Bertita was born she almost completely forgot about the others. Their mere memory horrified her, like something heinous that she had been forced to do. To Mazzini, although to a lesser degree, the same thing happened.

Not even the perfect child brought peace to their souls. From their first fight they had lost respect for each other; and if there was something to which man feels drawn to with cruel relish, it was, the cruel humiliation of a person they no longer respect. Before, they held back by mutual lack of success; now that success had arrived, each one, attributing it personally, felt the burden of the four monsters that the other had forced to create.

With these feelings, there was no longer any possible affection for the four oldest children. The maid dressed them, fed them, put them to bed, with visible brutality. They were hardly ever washed. They spent the whole day sitting in front of the fence, abandoned of any remote caress. In this way Bertita turned four years old, and that night, as a result of the sweets that the parents absolutely could not deny her, the child had some chills and fever. And the fear of seeing her die or be an idiot, reopened the eternal wound.

They hadn't spoken in three hours, and the reason was, as almost always, Mazzini's strong footsteps.

"My God! can you walk slower? How often …?"

"Well, I forget; I do not do it on purpose."

She smiled contemptuously: "No, I don't believe you so much!"

"Nor would I ever have believed you so much … Skinny woman!"

"What? What did you say?"

"Nothing!"

"Yes, I heard you say something! Look: I don't know what you said; but I swear to you that I prefer anything to have a father like the one you have!"

Mazzini went pale.

"Finally!" He murmured through clenched teeth. "At last, snake, you have said what you wanted!"

"Yes, snake, yes!" She said, "But I've had healthy parents, you hear, healthy! My father did not die of delirium! I would have had children like everyone else! Those are your sons, the four are yours!"

Mazzini exploded in turn.

"You snake! That's what I told you, what I want to tell you! Ask him, ask the doctor who is most to blame for your children's illness: my father or your punctured lung!"

They continued with increasing violence, until a moan from Bertita instantly sealed their mouths. By one o'clock in the morning the slight indigestion had disappeared, and as fatally happens with all young couples who have loved each other intensely even once, the reconciliation came.

A splendid day dawned, and as Berta got up, she spat blood. Emotions and last night were, without a doubt, at fault. Mazzini held her in his arms for a long time, and she cried desperately, but neither of them dared to say a word.

At ten they decided to leave for lunch. As they barely had time, they ordered the maid to kill a chicken.

The bright day had ripped the idiots from their bench. So, while the maid was slaughtering the animal in the kitchen, bleeding it slowly (Berta had learned this good way to preserve the freshness of meat from her mother), she thought she felt something breathing behind her. She turned, and saw the four idiots, their shoulders pressed against each other, staring at the operation in amazement ... "Red ... red ..."

"Berta! The children are here in the kitchen."

Berta arrived; she never wanted them to step there. And even in those hours of full forgiveness, forgetfulness, and regained happiness, that horrible vision could not be avoided! Because, naturally, the more intense was her love for her husband and daughter, the more irritated was her mood with the monsters.

"Throw them out, Maria! Throw them out! Throw them out, I say!"

The four poor creatures, shaken, brutally pushed, went to their bench.

After lunch, they all left. The maid went to Buenos Aires and the couple went for a walk through the villas. When the sun went down, they returned; but Berta wanted to say hello to her neighbors across the street. Her daughter ran home immediately.

Meanwhile the idiots had not moved all day from their bench. The sun had already crossed the fence, and was beginning to sink. They continued looking at the bricks, more inert than ever.

Suddenly something came between their gaze and the fence. Their sister, tired of five parental hours, wanted to get inside. Stopped at the foot of the fence, she looked thoughtfully at them. She wanted to climb, that offered no doubt. She decided on using a broken chair, but it wasn't high enough. She then resorted to a kerosene drawer, and her topographical instinct made her place the cabinet upright, with which she succeeded.

The four idiots, their gaze indifferent, saw how their sister patiently managed to master her balance, and how on tiptoes she rested her throat on the crest of the fence, between her taut hands. They saw her look everywhere, and seek support with her foot to lift herself higher.

But the look of the idiots had brightened; the same insistent light was fixed on their pupils. They did not take their eyes off their sister as a growing sense of bestial gluttony changed every line on their faces. Slowly they advanced toward the fence. The little girl, who, having managed to wedge her foot, was already going to straddle and fall on the other side, surely felt herself being caught by the leg. Beneath her, the eight eyes fixed on her scared her.

"Let go of me!" She yelled, shaking her leg.

"Mother! Ow mom! Mom! Dad!" She cried imperiously. She still tried to hold onto the edge, but she felt herself ripped away and fell.

"Mother! Ma..." She couldn't scream anymore. One of them squeezed her neck, removing her hairs as if they were feathers, and the others dragged her on one leg to the kitchen, where that morning the hen had been bled, tightly held, ripping her life second by second.

Mazzini, in the house opposite, thought he heard his daughter's voice.

"I think she's calling you," he said to Berta.

They listened uneasily, but heard no more. However, a moment later they said goodbye, and while Berta was putting down her hat, Mazzini advanced towards the patio.

"Bertita!"

No one answered.

"Bertita" He yelled.

And the silence was so funereal to his ever-terrified heart that his back froze with a horrible foreboding.

"My daughter, my daughter!" He ran desperately. But as he passed the kitchen, he saw a sea of blood on the floor. He violently pushed the door ajar, and uttered a cry of horror.

Berta, who ran at the same time when she heard the anguished call from the father, heard the cry and responded with another. But as she rushed into the kitchen, Mazzini, livid as death, intervened, restraining her:

"Don't come in. Don't come in!"

Berta could see the blood flooded floor. She could only throw her arms over her head and sink along with him with a hoarse sigh.

The Rubber Gloves

The individual became ill. He came home with an excruciating headache and nausea. He lay down, and in the gloomy stillness of the room, he felt relieved. Just three hours later, his condition worsened in such a way that he began to complain about a tight lip. The doctor came, already at night, and soon left, leaving the patient in darkness, with ice packs on his forehead.

The daughters of the house, naturally worried, told us in a still-low voice, in the dining room, that it was a stroke, but luckily it had been countered in time. Above all, the oldest of them, an intensely nervous, feeble, and disheveled girl, was deeply troubled. She fixed her gaze on each of her sisters, who said the same things.

"And you, Desdemona, have you seen him?" asked Ofelia.

"No! But I have heard his cries of pain. Is he pale?" She turned to Ofelia.

"Yes, but not at first. Now he has black lips."

The girls kept talking as Desdemona's wide eyes darted from side to side.

I suppose that the patient had a bad night because I found everyone in the dining room agitated the next day. What the patient had was not a stroke but smallpox. Unlike the previous diagnosis, the girls burned with optimism.

The doctor said to the mother: "Don't worry, madam, it is an extremely benign case."

Ofelia felt relieved. On the other hand, the older sister was mute, paler than usual, hanging on the eyes of the one who spoke.

"And smallpox can't be cured, right?" She dared to ask, deeply anxious that he would not be cured and that there were even worse things ahead.

"It's a completely benign case!" repeated the sisters, rosy with a prophetic spirit. Although hours later, they took the patient to the quarantine room. At night, we learned that he was still sick, with the most funereal black pox that is possible to acquire at customs. The next day men went to disinfect the room where the terrible thing had incubated, and three days later, the individual died, liquefied in hemorrhages.

Although our contact with the individual had been minimal, we did not live utterly calm until after seven days. The topic arose every day in the dining room, and as some knew about microbes at the table, they deemed every cough and touch suspicious.

Death, surely already habitual in Desdemona's nervous terrors, this time took a more tangible form.

"Oh, what a horror, the microbes!" Desdemona said as she closed her eyes. "To think that one is full of them ...

"Be careful with your hands, and you'll get rid of them."

"Not so much," argued another. "There have been infections by letter. Who is going to wash their hands to open an envelope?"

Ofelia's wild eyes were fixed on the last speaker. After a moment of terrifying reverie, she looked sharply at her hands. I do not know who had the misfortune to stir her up then.

Her insistence on looking at her hands developed her eyesight in such a way that little by little; she could see the microbes creeping up to her.

"How awful! Shut up!" cried Desdemona.

Days later, I stopped eating there, and a year later, I went one evening to see those people. I found the profound silence in the house quite disturbing; I found everyone gathered in the dining room, silent and red-eyed; Desdemona had died two days before. I immediately remembered the individual with smallpox.

The month after I stopped seeing them, Desdemona lived only by washing her hands. After each ablution, she carefully looked at her hands, satisfied with their sterility. Little by little, her eyes widened, and she understood well that after brief contact with the sleeve of her dress, the microbes from the terrible smallpox disease could be creeping up her hands. She kept going back to the sink, coming out of it after a quarter of an hour with reddened fingers. Ten minutes later, the microbes were crawling up again.

The mother—who, having read a novel before her marriage, still had a weakness for the most romantic of tales—came to find her daughter's distinguished fear excessive. The skin on her hands, terribly dry, was bright pink as if she were skinned.

The doctor pointed out to the young woman that it was a monomania—dangerous if you will—but in the end, just a monomania.

Desdemona nodded willingly, for she understood perfectly. She left satisfied. After laughing at herself with her sisters, she raised her bandaged hands to her eyes, with a deep sigh of relief at last.

"To think that I thought microbes were climbing…" She pondered as she continued looking at her hands. Little by little, her eyes widened. She finally shook her hands with a sharp movement and looked away, contracted, forcing herself to think of something else. Ten minutes later, her desperate brush was tearing her skin again.

For long months the madness continued, returning joyfully from the consulting rooms, permanently cured, and after two minutes of silent contemplation, running into the water.

She went to another doctor, who, more skeptical than his colleagues regarding fixed ideas, was very aware of subliminal suggestions. In pursuit of a careful examination of the hands in every way, he said to Desdemona, with a noticeably clear voice and eyes:

"Your skin is sick. Your brush mistreats it even more, so it must be treated."

And he wasted two hours touching the hand almost pore by pore with a syringe filled with solution A. Then, every ten contacts, a cotton ball soaked in solution B and silently pressed there for half a minute.

That day Desdemona was so happy that in the night, she woke up several times, without the slightest temptation to wash her hands, although she considered it frequently. But the next morning, she ripped all the bandages and headed to the bathroom.

Thus, the brush devoured the epidermis, leaving her raw skin exposed. The last doctor, informed of the previous failures, cured her, then enclosed her hands in hermetic rubber gloves, girded around the forearm with collodions and strips.

"In this way, he said, you can be sure that microbes cannot reach your hands. Furthermore, I must tell you that in the state of your hands, the slightest madness you do can lead you to lose them."

"I do know that it's just me being crazy. I'll be careful!" she laughed, confused.

And she was happy until the precise moment when it occurred to her that nothing was more possible than a microbe had been left inside. She desperately laughed out loud on the bed, trying to forget that thought. But after a while, the tip of the scissors tore a tiny hole in the gloves. As it was apparent to her that the microbe would come out of there, she lay down calmly. But then another thought crossed her mind. She thought that through the hole, many more microbes would enter.

The next morning the mother, restless, got up very early and found all the bloody bandages at the side of the basin. This time the microbes entered abruptly and mercilessly through her hands. I learned from Ofelia and Artemis that she endured five days of fever, followed by death.

The Lonely Man

Kassim was a sickly man, a jeweler by profession, who had no established shop. He worked for the big stores, his specialty being the assembly of precious stones. There existed few hands like his for the elaboration of delicate jewels. With more business skills, he would have been rich. But at thirty-five, he was still working from his living room.

Kassim, with a strong body, a bloodless face shadowed by a thin, black beard, had a beautiful and strongly passionate wife. The young woman, of street origin, had aspired with her beauty to a wealthy husband. She waited until she was twenty, provoking men and her neighbors with her body. Fearful at last, she hesitantly accepted Kassim.

No more luxury dreams, however. Her husband, still a skilled artist, lacked the character to make a fortune. For this reason, while the jeweler bended over his tweezers, she, on her elbows, held a slow and heavy gaze on her husband, then abruptly followed with her eyes behind the glass the high-standing passerby who could have been her husband.

Everything Kassim earned, however, was for her. On Sundays, he also worked hard, and the proceeds were all for her. When Maria wanted a jewel—and how passionately she wanted them! —he worked all night.

Little by little the daily dealings with the gems came to make her love the craftsman's tasks. But when the jewel was finished—it had to go; it wasn't for her—she fell deeper into the disappointment of her marriage. She tried on jewelry, pausing before the mirror. At last, she would leave it on and go to her room. Kassim would get up when he heard her sobs, and he would find her in bed, not wanting to speak with him.

"I do what I can for you," he said at last, sadly.

These situations were repeated so often that Kassim no longer got up to console her. Comfort her! Of what? Nothing mattered. Kassim continued working more and more, so he could provide more money to his beloved.

He was an indecisive, irresolute, and silent man. His wife's gazes now stopped with heavier fixation on his silent tranquility.

"And you are a man," she murmured.

Kassim did not cease to move his fingers.

"You're not happy with me, Maria," he said softly.

"Happy?! And you have the courage to say that. Who can be happy with you? Not even the last woman on Earth! Poor devil," she concluded with a nervous laughter as she left the room.

Kassim worked that night until three in the morning, and his wife then came across another object of her interest.

"Yes … It's an incredible headband … When did you make it?"

"Since Tuesday," he looked at her with faded tenderness, "while you were sleeping …"

"Oh, you could have gone to bed … huge, those diamonds!"

Her passion was the voluminous stones that Kassim crafted. He went on with his work with a mad hunger for it to be finished at once, and as soon as the jewelry was completed, she ran to the mirror with it. Then she would cry.

"Everyone, any husband, the last one, would make a sacrifice to flatter his wife! And you … and you … I don't even have a miserable dress to wear!"

When a certain limit of respect for the man is crossed, women can say incredible things to their husbands.

Kassim's wife crossed that line with a passion at least equal to that of her feeling towards fine diamonds. One afternoon, when putting away his jewelry, Kassim noticed the lack of a pin—five thousand pesos worth. He searched his drawers again.

"Haven't you seen the pin, Maria? I left it here."

"Yes, I saw it."

"Where is it?" he turned, puzzled.

"Right here!"

His wife, her eyes blazing and her mouth mocking, stood with the brooch on.

"It suits you very well," Kassim said after a while. "Let's put it away."

Maria laughed.

"Oh, no. It's mine!"

"Are you kidding?"

"Yes, just kidding! It really hurts to think that it could be mine … Tomorrow I will give it to you. Today I will go to the theater with it."

Kassim was shocked.

"That's wrong … They could see you. They would lose all trust in me."

"Oh!" she closed the door violently in angry annoyance.

Returning from the theater, she placed the jewel on the nightstand. Kassim got up and locked it in his workshop. When he returned, his wife was sitting on the bed.

"I mean, you are afraid I will steal it from you! That I am a thief!"

"Don't say that … You've been reckless, nothing more."

"Ah! And they entrust it to you! To you, to you! And when your wife asks you for a bit of flattery and wants a diamond, you call me a thief! How dare you!"

She slept at last, but Kassim didn't sleep.

They later delivered to Kassim the "solitary," the most precious diamond that had ever been through his hands.

"Maria, look. What a stone. I have never seen anything like it."

His wife said nothing. However, Kassim felt her breathe deeply because of the precious stone now in front of her.

"This is quite extraordinary. It will easily fetch nine or ten thousand pesos."

"A ring!" Maria finally replied.

"No, it's for a man … a pin."

Ten times a day she interrupted her husband to go try the diamond in front of the mirror. Later, she wore it with different dresses.

"Try it on later, Maria …" Kassim dared. "It's a rush job."

He waited in vain for a reply as his wife walked towards the balcony.

"Maria, they can see you!"

"Take it. Here's your damn stone!"

The stone, abruptly torn, rolled on the floor.

Kassim, livid, picked it up, examined it, then looked up from the ground at his wife.

"Well, why are you looking at me like that?" she asked. "Did something happen to your stone?"

"No," Kassim replied. And at once he resumed his hard work, although his hands were shaking in a pitiful manner.

But he had to get up at last to see his wife in the bedroom having a nervous breakdown. Her hair had come loose, and her eyes were bulging.

"Give me the diamond!" she cried. "Give it to me! We will run away! For me. Do it for me!"

"Maria …" Kasim said in a soft voice, trying to disengage.

"Ah!" roared his maddened wife. "You are the thief, you wretch! You have stolen my life, thief, thief! And you thought I wasn't going to get even … cuckold! Aha! Look at me … never occurred to you, huh? Ah!" And she put both hands to her own throat as if she would choke herself. When Kassim was leaving, she jumped out of bed and fell, reaching for him.

"Never mind! The diamond, give it to me! I don't want more than that! It's mine, miserable Kassim!"

Kasim helped her up.

"You're sick, Maria. We'll talk later. Please lay down."

"My diamond!"

"Ok, we'll see if it's possible for you to keep it. Now lay down."

"Give it to me!"

Kassim went back to work. As his hands had a mathematical security, there were only a few hours left to complete his arduous task.

Maria got up to eat, and Kassim went with her as usual. At the end of dinner, his wife looked at him straight ahead.

"It's a lie, Kassim." she said.

"Oh!" Kassim replied. "It's nothing."

"I swear it's a lie," she insisted.

Kassim smiled again, caressing her hand softly. He then stood up quietly to continue working on that precious stone. His wife followed him with her sight.

"And he won't tell me more than that …" she murmured. And with a deep nausea towards her sticky, flabby, and inert husband, she went to her room.

She didn't sleep well. She woke up, late now, and saw light in the workshop; her husband continued working. An hour later, her husband heard a scream.

"Give it to me!"

"Yes, it's for you; It won't take long, Maria," he said hastily, getting up. But his wife, after that nightmarish cry, was fast asleep.

At two in the morning, Kassim was able to finish his work; the diamond glowed firmly and beautifully. With a silent step, he went to the bedroom and lit a candle. Maria slept on her back, in the icy whiteness of her nightgown.

He went to the workshop and came back again. He stared at her almost exposed breast for a while, and with a faded smile, pushed the detached nightgown a little further.

His wife didn't feel it.

There wasn't much light. Kassim's face suddenly turned expressionless, like a stone. Suspending the jewel at the height of her naked breast for an instant, he plunged as firmly and perpendicularly as a nail the entire pin into her heart.

There was a sharp opening of the eyes, followed by a slow drooping of the eyelids. Her fingers arched, and nothing else.

The jewel, shaken by the convulsion of the wounded woman, trembled for a moment unbalanced. Kassim waited a moment; and when the diamond was at last perfectly still, he was then able to leave, closing the door behind him without making a sound.

The Puritan

The cinematographer's workshops, those studios around which millions of faces revolve in an orbit of never-satisfied curiosity and dreams never accomplished, have inherited from the abandoned painting workshop the legend of incredible feats on the altar of art.

On the one hand, the freedom of spirit familiar to great actors, and on the other, the very rich salaries that they earn, explain these festivals that not infrequently have the sole purpose of keeping the audience vibrant, before the fantastic, distant Hollywood stars.

Once the day's work is complete, everyone leaves the studio. Perhaps the technical employees continue their work throughout the night, and maybe one or ten kilometers away, the daily tumult continues in a party. But on the sets, in the studio proper, the silence now reigns.

This silence and the appearance of emptiness are traits of the central wardrobe, a vast hall whose façade, so broad that it would give way to three cars, opens onto the interior patio, onto the sizeable sand—grained square with all the workshops.

The cloakroom lies at the end of the square, and its large gate always remains open. Through the many leaves, on clear nights, the moon invades much of the dark hall. In that quiet room, where no soul can even hear the screeching of the loudest machines, we have our gathering late at night of the dead actors of the films.

The photographic impression on the tape, shaken by the speed of the machines, excited by the burning light of the spotlights, galvanized by the ongoing projection, has deprived our sad bones of the peace that should reign over them. We are dead, without a doubt, but our destruction is not total. An intangible survival, barely warm so as not to be made of ice, governs and animates our specters. Through the wardrobe, in peace, we wander in the light of the moon, without anxiety, without passions or memories. Something like a vague stupor hangs over our movements. We would seem like sleepwalkers, indifferent to each other, if the immediate gloom of the enclosure did not pretend a vague hall of a mansion, where the ghosts of what we have been continue a passable imitation of life.

We have not shaken the souls of the artists that survive us in vain; We have not let our hearts sleep in their arms a hundred times so that their present films are not the nocturnal commentary of our conciliators. Our own past—life, struggles, and love—is closed to us. Our existence starts with a camera shutter. We are an instant: perhaps imperishable, but a single spectral instant. The film and the projection deprived us of our eternal sleep, closed the world to us, off the screen, to any other interest.

Our gathering does not always bring together, however, all the visitors of the cloakroom. When someone misses the meeting, we already know that some theater is displaying one of his films.

"He's sick," we say. "He has stayed home."

The next night, or three or four later, the ghost returns to his usual place in the company he prefers. And although his countenance expresses fatigue and the fine ravages of a new projection are perceived in his silhouette, there are no traces of actual suffering in them.

It seems that during the time of the passage of the film, the actor fell into a state of semi-consciousness.

A very different thing happened with Ella (I don't want to provide her real name), the beautiful and vivid star, who one night made her entrance among us—dead.

The success that this actress achieved in life in her brilliant and fleeting meteor career is not news to anyone. Of any woman, she possessed the most decadent qualities. The extreme beauty of the face, of her body, of her soul—

any one of these supreme gifts can by itself bring down a feminine soul with her excessive charm. She, almost as a punishment, possessed and endured all three.

She possessed everything in her brief passage through the world. She knew the follies of success, fortune, vanity, flattery, danger. Faith only denied her the foolishness of love.

Among all the men who surrendered to her, by her very side or through two thousand leagues of clamor and desire, she offered herself entirely to the only being capable of rejecting her: a puritan of inviolable moral principles, who before meeting the actress had placed his honor on his wife and their tender ten-month-old son.

It was not easy to guess the state of her feelings, but it would not have been pleasant for anyone to bear the shock that her simple principles freed in her heart with her guilty love.

She had met him in the studio, for the lucky mortal had a deep interest in movies. And although she had never reached out to stretch her lips to him, she knew well that, had she done so, he would have removed her arms from his neck, stiff and rigid as duty itself.

She knew well that he loved her, but not as a man, but as a hero. And when a lover usurps for himself all the heroism of love, the other has nothing left but to die.

In short: the married man returned, bitter to the dregs, the cup of love that she held out to him with her body. And she, without the strength to resist, killed herself.

Suicidal, indeed, she could not enjoy peace, nor had her love and pain been forbidden to her. Her heart always beat, and in her eyes, deeply excavated, we could not guess what dose of arsenic or mortal love was still dilating them with anguish.

Because contrary to what happened with us, she lived a half-life. When a theater plays our films, we disappear from the gathering, as I have already mentioned. She does not. She was lying right there, wrapped in cold, her expression anxious and panting. We pretended not to notice her presence in such cases, but she sat up on the couch when the projection barely finished. She then expressed to us her distress.

"Oh, what anguish!" She told us, uncovering her forehead. "I'm sorry for everything I do as if I hadn't acted in the studio. Before, I knew that at the end of a scene, no matter how strong it might have been, I could think of something else and laugh. Not anymore! It's like I'm the character myself!"

Well. We had reached the end of our days, and we didn't owe anything to anybody. Ella cut her days short. Her unfinished life suffered a substantial deficit, her feigned pain.

She had to pay. Of her love, she had said nothing to us, until the night when at the end of her task she murmured bitterly:

"If only ... if only I could stop seeing him!"

Oh! We didn't need to remember either. For us to understand the suffering of the poor creature: night after night, after a month of complete disappearance from Hollywood, Mac Namara attended from the stalls of the theater, and without missing one, the films of Ella.

Never until today has literature taken full advantage of the extraordinary situation that occurred when a husband, a son, a mother, tun to see on the screen, throbbing with life, the loved one they lost. But neither was torture equal to that of a lover who finally sees herself surrender to the man for whom she killed herself. Who cannot run into his arms deliriously, cannot look at him, or even turn to him because all of her and their love are no longer more than a photographic spectrum.

Nor was it happiness what passed through the heart of the Puritan, whose wife and son slept peacefully but whose open eyes contemplated the actress alive.

For us, however, only Ella's situation was of lively interest. It is unfortunate to have died in vain when life still demands what it can no longer give.

"It is not possible," She sometimes murmured after seeing him leave, "to suffer more than I suffer!" Three-quarters of an hour watching him in the audience ...! And me here…!"

Insensibly, we had all forgotten our walks in the moonlight and our whispers without heat, to only contemplate that torment. We had a dark feeling that Ella could not resist the tortures she continued to inflict on herself with cruelty.

"Oh, die! And never to see him again!" She said to herself, pressing her face in her hands.

But Dougald Mac Namara did not take his eyes off Ella on the other side of the screen.

One night, at the sad hour, while Ella lay motionless on the couch, half-hidden by how many blankets we had been able to throw on her body, the young woman suddenly took her hands away from her eyes.

"He's not ..." she said slowly. "Today, he has not come."

The film's screening continued, but the actress no longer seemed to suffer from the passion of her characters. Everything had vanished into inert nothingness, leaving in compensation a path of livid and tremendous anguish, which went from an empty armchair to a ghostly couch.

Neither the next night, nor the next, nor those that followed for a month, Dougald Mac Namara returned.

Must I warn that from half an hour before the exhibition on all those nights, our lips remained mute and that from the first squeak of the film, our eyes did not leave Ella?

She was also waiting—and in what way!—From the very beginning of the projection. For a long time—the time of looking for him in the living room—her face, thinned by suicide, looked fantastic with eager hope. And when her eyes finally closed—Mac Namara hadn't come!

New nights followed, in vain. Nobody now occupied the usual seat of the theater.

In an austere home, a man of rigid principles must have watched over the dream of his chaste wife and his pure infant. When he has resisted a warm mouth that begs for a kiss, he opposes a dancing celluloid illusion very well. After a moment of weakness, Mac Namara would no longer return to the Monopole.

We believed so. Ella no longer expressed her wish to die; she was dying.

One night, finally, shortly after the projection began, and while we did not lose sight of her face, she separated her dead hands abruptly from her face.

Suddenly her face lit up with happiness to that radiant splendor that only life has the secret, and reaching out her arms; she cried out. But what a scream, oh God!

"She has seen him!" we said to ourselves. "He has returned to the Monopole!"

It was more. Over there, somewhere in the world, the rigidly principled Puritan had just shot himself.

So there is something superior to Death and Duty. Two steps from us, now, the lovers are close. The lovers won't ever be separated. He stifled his impure love, was temporarily defeated when he went to hide in the theater and returned at last in triumph to his austere home. He sits now next to her, on the couch.

She smiles in almost carnal bliss, pure as her death. She no longer owes nothing to destiny, and she rests in peace. She has fulfilled her wish.

The White Syncope

I was ready for anything except ingesting chloroform.

I am from a family in which heart disease has passed from father to son with grim persistence. Some of my relatives were lucky, and according to the surgeon who operated on me, I enjoyed that privilege. The truth is that he and his colleagues examined me conscientiously, their unanimous opinion being that my heart could be considered as good overall as my liver and my kidneys. There was no choice for me but to let them put on the mask and entrust my sacred entrails to the scalpel.

So I gave up, and one autumn afternoon, I found myself lying with my nose and lips full of Vaseline, eagerly inhaling chloroform as if I was short of air. Yes, there was no air, and there was chloroform that came in jets of unbearable sweetness: jets of candy through the nose, through the mouth, through the ears. The saliva, the lungs, the tips of the fingers, all were nauseous.

I began to lose track of things, and what I last remember was, on a black background, gleaming snow crystals.

I was in heaven. If I wasn't, it looked very much like it. My first impression, coming back to me, was that I had died.

"This is heaven!" I told myself. Down there, who knows where and at what distance I died due to the operation. In an infinite and lost room on Earth, which is just a remote little light in space, lies my lifeless body, my body that yesterday had triumphantly escaped the doctors' examination. Now that body stays there; I have nothing more to do with it anymore. I am in heaven; I live because I am a living soul.

But I still saw myself in human form, on a white and polished floor. Where was I then? I observed the place. The view did not go beyond a hundred meters, as a dense mist closed the horizon in the area covered by my eyes. In front of me, 30 or 40 meters, stood a white building that looked like a Greek temple. To my left, vanished in the mist, rose another similar structure.

Where was I? Besides me, and emerging from behind, beings passed through, human persons like me, who were heading to the opposite building, where they entered. And other people were leaving, undertaking the same way back. Farther on to the left, the same phenomenon repeated itself, from the unfathomable mist to the smoldering temple. What was that? Who were those persons who did not know each other, didn't even look at each other, on the same sleepwalking path?

When I began to find everything a little out of the ordinary, even for heaven, I heard a voice say to me:

"What are you doing here?"

I turned and saw a man in a guard's uniform, with a cap and a short stick in his hand. I saw him well in his human figure, but I'm not sure he was entirely opaque.

"I don't know," I answered, puzzled myself. "I find myself here, not knowing how."

"Well, you should be over there," said the guard, pointing to a building. "That is where you should go. Have you not had surgery?"

Instantly, in an immemorial remoteness of time and space, I found myself lying on a table—in a very remote past.

"Indeed," I murmured hazily. "I have been—I had surgery... And I've died." The guard shook his head.

"They all say the same thing ... You give us more work than you imagine ... Haven't you had time to read the inscription yet?"

"What inscription?"

"In that building," the warden pointed out with his short stick.

I looked in surprise towards the Greek temple, and with even greater surprise, I read on the frontispiece, in prominent characters of filtered light:

BLUE SYNCOPE

"This is your waiting area for now," the guard said. "Everyone who falls into syncope during a chloroform operation waits there. So let's go because you should have your number assigned by now."

Disturbed, I headed to the building in question as the guard accompanied me.

"Very well," I finally told him when I arrived. "I will enter here, as I have fallen into syncope, but what about that other building?"

"That? It's the same thing, almost. Read the sign. I've never seen one of you chloroformed people read the signs. What does it say? You can go ahead and read it."

And it read:

WHITE SYNCOPE

"That's right," the man confirmed. "White Syncope. Those who enter there do not leave anymore because they have fallen into white syncope. Do you understand at last?"

I didn't quite understand, so the guard lost another minute explaining everything to me, pointing from one building to another.

According to him, chloroformed products have two dangers, independent of cut glass or other operation complications. In one of the cases, and when inhaling the first mouthful of chloroform, the patient suddenly loses consciousness; a deathly paleness invades the countenance; and the sick man, with his wax lips and his paralyzed heart, is ready for burial.

It is white syncope.

The other danger manifests itself in the course of the operation. The face from the chloroform suddenly flushed; the lips, gums, and tongue become purple, and if the individual's body is not strong enough to react against intoxication, death ensues.

It's the blue syncope.

As can be seen, the person falls into this last syncope and has his life hanging by a very fine thread. He indeed still lives, but he is already feeling the abyss of death with his foot.

"You are in this state," the guard concluded. "And you must go there. If you are lucky and the surgeons manage to revive you, you will go out again through the same door. But, for the moment, wait there. However, those who go in there," he pointed to the other building, "do not go out anymore. However, those who fall into white syncope are few and far between."

"But," I objected, "every two or three minutes, I see one come in."

"Because they come from all over the world. How many operated people do you think there are at any given time? You don't know, and neither do I. But look instead at those who enter here."

Indeed, our path was a constant coming and going, a continuous column of men, women, and children, entering and leaving in order and without haste. The peculiarity of that avenue of ghost-beings was the total ignorance in which they seemed to be of each other. They did not know each other, nor did they look at each other, nor did they perhaps see each other. Instead, they passed by with their usual expression, perhaps distracted or thinking about something, probably with concerns of everyday life—business or domestic details—the expression of people leaving a train station.

Before entering, I glanced at the visitors of the White Syncope. They, too, seemed to realize what the Greek temple vanished in the mist meant. They went to their deaths dressed in jackets or feminine blouses, with trivial concerns of the life they had just abandoned.

And this railway station-looking mundane aspect became more sensitive as I entered the Blue Syncope. The guard left me at the gate, where a new guard, more hurried than the previous one, cried out loud my number: 834, as he put his palm on my shoulder to get me inside at once.

The interior was a single hall, a long room with benches in the center and sides. The overhead light, very dim, and even the slight haze of the environment, reinforced the impression of a waiting room late at night. Several people occupied the benches who came in and sat down to wait, resigned to an unavoidable procedure as if it were a merely inevitable setback. Most did not even lean against the back of the bank; patients were waiting, brooding over some trivial concern. Others leaned back and closed their eyes to kill time. Finally, some relied on their knees and put their faces in their hands.

No one—and I was still astonished—seemed to be aware of what this waiting meant. Nobody spoke. You could only hear the visitors' clear passage in the hall and the guards' voices yelling the numbers in order. Hearing them, the owners of the numbers got up and went out the front door. But not all of them, because another door was also wide open at the other end of the room, with a guard yelling other numbers.

The owners of these numbers got up with the same indifference as the others and walked to said back door.

Some, especially people waiting with their eyes closed or with their faces in their hands, mistakingly went to another door. But before the guard said another number, they noticed their error and went with some haste to the right door. The guard did not always tell the number either; if the person were close or looked distracted, the guard would whistle to indicate the destination with his finger.

"Was the back door then for...?" Then, for greater certainty, I went to that door and approached the guard.

"Excuse me," I said. "Can you tell me what specific meaning this door has?"

The guard, apparently quite annoyed with his duties to take over those of the public, looked at me as a station worker would look at the subject who asked him if he was in the right station.

"Excuse me," I said again. "I have the right to be informed by employees correctly."

"Very well," said the guard, touching his cap and standing to his feet. "What do you want to know?"

"What this door means."

"Right away; those who have died walk through this door."

"Those who die ...?"

"Not everyone who dies. Only those who have died in syncope."

"In the Blue Syncope?"

"So it seems."

I did not ask any more questions, and I went to the door; beyond there, I could see nothing; all was darkness, and there was a very unpleasant impression of freshness.

I retraced my steps and sat down. Beside me, a young woman in a dark suit waited with her eyes closed and her head leaning on the back of the bench. I looked at her for a long time and leaned in with my face in my palms.

I knew that the guards would say my number at any moment, but besides this, I had just looked at the young woman in the short skirt and the priestesses who in a tiny operating room had just fallen into syncope like me. And never, in the short days of my previous life, had I seen a beauty more remarkable than that of that pale and distracted enchantment on the edge of death.

I raised my head and fixed my gaze on her again. Then, finally, she opened her eyes and looked from one guard to the other as if surprised that they did not call her. Then, when she was going to close her eyes again, I said:

"Are you nervous?"

She turned her eyes to me, looked at me for a brief moment, and smiled:

"A little."

She wanted to go numb again, but I told her something else. What did I tell her? What thirst for beauty and adoration was there in my soul when I found a way to talk to that earthly love?

I do not know, but for three-quarters of an hour—if we can count earthly time on the ecstasy of our ghosts—our voices, our eyes, spoke incessantly.

And without being able to exchange a single promise, because neither she nor I knew our mutual names, nor did we know if we would revive, nor in what place on Earth we had walked one day with firm feet.

Would I see her again? Was our old world big enough to hide from my eyes that beloved creature, who gave me her paralyzed heart in the limbo of the Blue Syncope? No. I would see her again— because she did not doubt that she was coming back to life. So when the guard said her number, and she walked to the door, waking up with a smile, I followed her with my eyes as if she were my fiancée.

What's going on? Why did they stop her? New employees appear suddenly—bosses, indeed—who observe the order number of the young woman. Then, at last, they let her go, with a gesture that I cannot understand. And I hear something like:

"Another mistake ... We will have to watch the guards below ..."

What mistake? And who are the guards below? I sit down again, indifferent to the nightly swaying, when the guard at the back door shouts: 124!

My neighbor, a man with an energetic face, a businessman, gets up indifferently as if he were going to his office like every other day. And in that instant, upon hearing his number, I feel for the first time the possibility that they might call me from *the other door*.

Is it possible? But she just got up, and I see her still smiling at me, with her short dress and her translucent stockings. And before a second, less perhaps, I can stand still from her forever and ever in the most infinite ever that establishes an open door, behind which there is no more darkness and a very unpleasant feeling of coolness. From which door will they shout my number? To which door should I turn my eyes? What bored guardian will nod me to my destiny?

* * *

I did not come to my senses; everything was still buzzing with chloroform. Then, finally, I opened my eyes and saw the white ghosts that had just operated on me.

One of them patted me on the shoulder, saying:

"Try to be in less of a hurry to pass out again, my friend. Anyway, you should be delighted."

But I did not hear him because I had fallen into inactivity again. So when I woke up, I was already in bed.

In bed...? In a sanatorium ...? In the world, isn't this ...? That had only been, was, and would be my life from now on. But the light, the smell of formol, the metallic noises—life as it is—damaged my eyes and soul. So far away, an eternity of time and space separating us was the young woman. How to find her among the thousand sanatoriums of the world?

The time! Yes! Only that precise data had and could be enough for me. He should start looking for her right away, in the sanitarium itself. Who knows? She might be there.

I called the doctor, my trusted doctor who had attended the operation.

"Listen to me, Fitzsimmons," I murmured. "I have a great interest in knowing if other people have undergone surgery in this sanatorium at the same time as me."

"Here? Are you extremely interested in knowing this?"

"Very much. At the same time, or a moment earlier, if anything."

"But yes, I think so ... Do you want to know for sure?"

"Please do me this favor..."

When I was alone, I closed my eyes again because what I wanted to see was very different from the lacquered bed's stark reflections.

"I can tell you," Fitzsimmons told me, walking back inside. "Three people have undergone surgery at the same time as you: two men and one woman. The men..."

"No, Fitzsimmons; only the woman interests me. Have you seen her?"

"Perfectly. But..." Fitzsimmons stopped, looking into my eyes, "what devil of a nightmare did you have while on chloroform?"

"It's not a nightmare ... I'll explain later! Listen to me: did you see her well? Can you describe her for me in detail?"

Fitzsimmons had seen her well, and I had no doubt. It was her. Despite life and death and the vastness of worlds, the girl was by my side! Alive, tangible, as she was in a distant past, infinitely earlier, in the dim light of an outer waiting room.

The doctor saw my change of expression and bit his lip.

"Did you know her?"

"Yes! Is she alright?"

He hesitated for a moment. He later said:

"I don't know if that young woman is the one you think." But the patient we operated on is now dead.

"Dead!"

"Yes ... We had little luck in the sanitarium today. You, who almost left us, and that girl, with a syncope."

"Blue," I murmured.

"No, white."

"White? No, blue! I became terrified. I am sure...!"

But my doctor exclaimed:

"I don't know where you get your diagnoses from now ... White syncope, I tell you, the most sudden one. And calm down now. Abandon the chloroform dreams that will lead you to nothing."

White Syncope! I was alone again. Suddenly there was light: I went to see those in charge of the waiting room, checking the number of the young woman, and I now appreciated in their total reach the words that at that moment had confused me: "There has been a mistake ..."

The mistake was that the girl had died on the operating table, from white syncope; that she had entered the waiting room dead, by the error of some guard; and that I had been in love to a deceased young woman, who by chance was smiling at me and still crossing her feet.

I have undoubtedly walked the same streets that she did during my life, perhaps with seconds of difference; we have possibly lived on the same block and probably on different floors of the same house. And we have never, ever met! So what life denied us is now granted by something unknown, since by mistake, I have overturned all the love of my oscillating life on a distant memory, now nothing but a cold corpse.

Whether what the doctor tells me is true or not, I always see her waking up with a smile, ready to wait for me when I close my eyes. When I left the room, she turned to the right to enter the White Syncope. She will never come out again. But it does not matter; there she waits for me, I'm sure.

Good. This sanatorium room, these hard angles, and this lacquered bed, are they real? Have I come back to life, or are my awakening and the conversation with my doctor just new syncopal dreaming forms? Isn't another mistake by the guards possible for me, consecutive to the one that has diverted my Dead-Bride to the right? Have I not been dead myself for a long time, waiting in the Blue Syncope for the control that the bosses carry out with my number again?

She left and entered calmly into the white building, before which all human illusion must retreat. No one on Earth will ever see her again.

But I? Is this lacquered bed real, or do I dream of it from the Great Shadow, where the bosses finally make way for me irritated by the unknown error, pointing out the White Syncope, where I should have been for a long time ...?

The Wild Honey

I have two cousins in Salto Oriental, now men, who at the age of twelve, and as a result of a great admiration for Jules Verne, gave in to the rich undertaking of leaving their home to go live in the mountains. This is six miles from the city. They would live primitively from hunting and fishing. It is true that the two boys had not particularly remembered to carry shotguns or hooks, but still, the forest was there, with its freedom as its source of joy and its dangers as its charm.

Benincasa, having completed his studies in public accounting, felt an overwhelming desire to learn about life in the jungle. He was not carried away by his temper, for rather Benincasa was a peaceful boy, plump and rosy-faced, on account of his excellent health. Consequently, sane enough to prefer tea with milk and cupcakes to who knows what random and hellish food he could find in the jungle. But just as the bachelor believes in his duty, on the eve of his wedding, to say goodbye to his free life with a night of orgy with his friends, Benincasa wanted to honor his old self with two or three shocks of intense life. And for this reason, he traveled up the Paraná to a construction site, wearing his expensive rain boots.

As soon as he left Corrientes, he had put on his sturdy boots, since the snakes on the shore were already close enough. But despite this, the public accountant took great care of his footwear.

In this way he arrived at the construction site of his godfather, who at the time had to stop the carelessness of his godson.

"Where are you going now?" he asked, surprised.

"To the mountain; I want to walk a bit," said Benincasa, who had just slung the Winchester over his shoulder.

"What!? You will not be able to take a step there. Follow the downstream, if you must … or better, leave that weapon, and tomorrow I'll have you accompanied by a worker."

Benincasa gave up his walk. Nevertheless, he went to the edge of the jungle and stopped. He hesitantly stepped inside and stood still. He shoved his hands into his pockets. After looking back at the jungle on both sides, he returned quite disappointed.

The next day, however, he ventured into the jungle for a few miles, and although his rifle returned intact, Benincasa did not deplore the walk. His prey would arrive in time.

His prey arrived on the second night—although in a different manner than he expected.

Benincasa was sleeping soundly when he was awakened by his godfather.

"Hey, sleepyhead! Get up! They're going to eat you alive."

Benincasa sat down abruptly on the bed, amazed by the light from the three wind lanterns moving from side to side in the room. His godfather and two workers watered the floor.

"What's going on? What's going on?" he asked, getting on the floor.

"Nothing … Watch out for your feet …"

Benincasa was already aware of the curious ants in the area. They are small, black, shiny insects that march swiftly along wide rivers. They are essentially carnivorous. They devour everything they find in their path: spiders, crickets, scorpions, toads, snakes, and many other beings. Their entry into a house means the absolute extermination of every living being, since there is no corner or deep hole where the devouring insects can't reach. The dogs howl, the oxen moo, and it is necessary to abandon the house, in exchange for not being gnawed in ten hours to the skeleton. They stay in one place for one, two, up to five days, depending on the richness in insects, meat, or fat. Once everything is eaten, they leave.

They do not resist, however, creolin or similar substances, and since in the construction site those chemicals abound, within an hour the site was free from those ants.

Benincasa observed very closely, on his feet, the livid sign of a bite.

"They bite really hard!" he said surprised, looking up at his godfather.

The latter, for whom the observation no longer had any value, did not respond, congratulating himself instead on having contained the invasion in time. Benincasa resumed sleep, albeit startled all night by tropical nightmares.

The next day he went to the mountains, this time with a machete, as he had concluded that such a tool would be much more useful in the mountains than his rifle.

It is true that his pulse was not wonderful, and his accuracy, much less so. But he still managed to chop the branches, whip his face, and scratch his boots, all in one.

The silent mountain soon tired him. In the bustling tropical life, there were at that hour only small insects, not an animal, not a bird, not a sound almost. Benincasa was returning when a buzzing sound caught his attention. Ten meters from him, in a hollow log, tiny bees circled the entrance to the hole. He approached cautiously and saw at the bottom of the opening ten or twelve dark balls, the size of eggs.

"This is honey," the accountant said out loud with intimate gluttony. "They must be wax bags, filled with honey …"

But between Benincasa and the bags were the bees. After a moment's rest, he thought of fire; it would raise a good smoke. As luck would have it, as the thief cautiously approached the succulent honey, four or five bees landed on his hand, without stinging him. Benincasa took one immediately, and pressing its abdomen, found that it had no stinger. Its saliva, already light, cleared in mellifluous abundance. Wonderful and good little animals!

In an instant the accountant detached the wax bags, and moving a long way to escape the sticky contact of the bees, he sat down on a stump. Of the twelve balls, seven contained pollen. But the rest were full of honey, a dark honey of somber transparency, which

Benincasa savored greedily. It tasted distinctly of something. To what? The accountant couldn't pin it down. Perhaps to fruit or eucalyptus resin.

Benincasa, once certain that the five little bags would be useful to him, began to eat. His idea was simple: have the dripping honeycomb suspended over his mouth. But since the honey was thick, he had to enlarge the hole, after having stood for half a minute with his mouth open uselessly. Then the honey leaked out, thinning into a heavy thread to the accountant's tongue.

One after another, the five combs were thus emptied into Benincasa's mouth.

Meanwhile, the sustained head-up position had made him a bit dizzy. Heavy with honey, still, and eyes wide open, Benincasa appreciated the twilight mountain again. The trees and the ground took overly oblique postures, and his head accompanied the swaying of the landscape.

"What a curious dizziness ..." thought the accountant. "And the worst part is ..."

As he got up and tried to take a step, he had been forced to fall back onto the stump. His body felt as heavy as lead, especially his legs, as if they were immensely swollen. And his hands and feet tingled.

"This is weird, very weird!" Benincasa repeated stupidly, without, however, scrutinizing the reason for this oddity. "Almost as if there were ants here."

And suddenly his breath stopped short with horror.

"It must be the honey! It's poisonous! I'm poisoned!"

And with a second effort to get up, his hair stood on end with terror; he hadn't even been able to move. Now the sensation of lead and tingling rose to his waist. For a time, the horror of dying there, miserably alone, far from his mother and friends, inhibited all means of defense.

"I'm going to die now ... In a while I'm going to die ... I can't move my hand!"

In his panic, he found, however, that he had no fever or sore throat, and that his heart and lungs maintained their normal rhythm. His anguish changed shape.

"I'm paralyzed; it's paralysis! And they won't find me!"

But an invincible drowsiness began to take hold of him, leaving his mental faculties intact. He thought he felt the swaying ground turn black and shake vertiginously. Again, the thought of the ants rose to his memory, and in his thoughts, he fixed as a supreme anguish the possibility that the black that was invading the ground was ...

He still had the strength to tear himself away from this last horror, and suddenly he uttered a cry, a true scream, in which the man's voice regained the tone of a terrified child: a precipitous river of black ants was climbing up his legs. Around him the devouring ants darkened the floor, and the accountant felt, under his pants, the river of carnivorous ants rising.

His godfather finally found, two days later, and without the slightest particle of flesh, a skeleton covered in Benincasa's clothes.

It is not common for wild honey to have such narcotic or paralyzing properties, but it can happen. Flowers with the same properties abound in the tropics, and the honey's taste already denounces its properties in most cases, such as the taste of eucalyptus resin that Benincasa thought he tasted.

The Son

It is a powerful summer day in Misiones, with all the sun, heat, and calm that the season can bring.

"Be careful, little one," the father says to his son, abridging in that sentence all the past occurrences that his son understands perfectly.

"Yes, Papa," the creature replies as he takes the shotgun and loads the pockets of his shirt with cartridges, which he closes carefully.

"Come back for lunch," the father said.

"Yes, Papa," the boy repeats.

He balances the shotgun in his hand, smiles at his father, kisses him on the head, and departs. His father follows him for a while with his eyes and goes back to work.

He knows that since his son was brought up from his earliest childhood in habit and caution from danger, he can handle a rifle and hunt no matter what. Although he is very tall for his age, he is only thirteen years old; he seems to be younger, judging by his blue eyes' purity, with childish surprise. He does not need his father to raise his eyes from his work to follow with his mind the march of his son.

He has crossed the red trail and is heading straight up the mountain through the open plains.

Hunting in the bush—fur game—requires more patience than his son can yield. After crossing that mountain, his son will go along the edge of the cacti, in search of pigeons, toucans, or herons, such as those that his friend Juan had found days before. Only now, the father smiles at the memory of the hunting passion of the two creatures. They only sometimes hunt a crow, a surucuá—even less often—and they return in triumph, Juan to his ranch with the nine-millimeter rifle that his father has given him, and his son to the plateau with the great Saint-Étienne shotgun, 16 gauge, quadruple lock and white powder.

He was the same. At thirteen, he would have given his life to own a shotgun. His son, of that age, owns it now, and the father smiles.

It is not easy, however, for a widowed father, with no other faith or hope than the life of his son, to educate him as he has done, sure of his little hands and feet since he was four years old, aware of the immensity of certain dangers and the unreliability of his strength.

That father had to fight hard against what he considers his selfishness. So quickly, a father miscalculates, allows a child to do something reckless, and loses a child!

The danger always exists for a man at any age, but the threat diminishes if he grows accustomed to having nothing to count on but his strength. In this way, the father has correctly educated his son. And to achieve this, he had to resist not only his heart but his moral torments; because the father, with a weak stomach and eyes, has been suffering from hallucinations for some time.

He has seen, embodied in the most painful illusion, memories of happiness that should have arisen out of the nothing in which he was secluded. The image of his son has not escaped this torment. He had once seen him roll wrapped in blood when the boy fired the shotgun in his workshop, being so what he did, in reality, was to work on the buckle of his hunting belt.

Horrible, horrible. But today, on this burning summer day, the father, who deeply loves his son, feels happy, calm, and assured of the future.

At that moment, not far away, he hears a boom.

"The Saint-Étienne shotgun" murmurs the father, recognizing the detonation—"two fewer pigeons in the bush."

Paying no more attention to the inconsequential event, the man absorbs himself again in his task.

The sun, already high, continues to climb. Wherever one looks—stones, earth, trees—the rarefied air as in a furnace vibrates with heat. A deep hum that fills the entire being and permeates the area as far as the eye can see concentrates all tropical life at that time.

The father glances at his wrist: twelve. And he lifts his eyes to the mountain. His son should be back by now. In the mutual trust they place in each other—the silver-tempted father and the thirteen-year-old child—they never deceive each other. When the son responds to him: "Yes, Dad", he will do what he says. He said that he would be back before twelve, and the father smiled when he saw him leave. And he has not returned.

The man goes back to his work, trying to focus his attention on his task. Is it so easy to lose track of time inside the forest and sit for a while on the ground while resting motionless?

More time has passed; it is half-past twelve. The father leaves his workshop, and as he rests his hand on the mechanical bench, the explosion of a parabellum bullet rises from the depths of his memory. Instantly, for the first time, he thinks that after the explosion of the Saint-Étienne, he has not heard anything. His son has not returned, and nature is stopped at the edge of the forest, waiting for him.

Oh! A temperate character and a blind trust in a child's education are not enough to chase away the specter of doom that a father with sick eyes sees rising from the mountain line. Distraction, forgetfulness, fortuitous delay: none of these small reasons that could delay the arrival of his child found a place in his heart.

One shot, he only heard one shot, and it was a long time ago. Besides it, the father has not heard a noise, has not seen a bird, has not seen a single person come to announce that a great misfortune...

Head in the air, and without a machete, the father goes. He enters the mountain, coasts the line of cacti without finding the slightest trace of his son.

But nature goes unopposed. And when the father has walked the familiar hunting trail, he acquires the assurance that every step he takes after that leads him, fatally and inevitably, to the corpse of his son.

Reproaching didn't do him any good. Only the cold, terrible, and consumed reality: his son has died somewhere. But where? There are so many fields there, and the mountain is so, so rocky! Oh, very rocky! His son might have not been careful when crossing a barbed wire with the shotgun in his hand.

The father stifles a cry. He has seen something rise in the distance. Oh, it is not his son, no! He then turns to another side, and another and another.

Nothing would be gained by seeing the color of his complexion and the anguish in his eyes. That man has not called his son yet. Although his heart cries out for him, his mouth remains mute. He knows well that the very act of pronouncing the name will be the confession of his death.

"My son!"—Suddenly escapes him. And if the voice of a man of character is capable of crying, let us cover our ears with mercy before the anguish that can be heard in the father's voice.

No one and nothing answered. Through the red bites of the sun, the father goes looking for his son, who, he presumes, has just died.

"My son ...! My little boy..!" He calls out in a diminutive that rises from the bottom of his insides.

Some time ago, in complete happiness and peace, the father had suffered the hallucination of his son rolling with his forehead open by a nickel-chrome bullet. Now, in every shadowy corner of the forest, he sees flashes of wire; and at the foot of a pole, with the unloaded shotgun beside him, he sees something.

"My son!"

The forces that allow a poor hallucinating father to be delivered to the most heinous nightmare also have a limit. And it feels that those forces are evading him when he abruptly sees his son in the distance, sitting next to the barbed wire.

It is enough for a thirteen-year-old boy to see his father's expression inside the mountain to hasten his step with wet eyes from fifty meters.

"My son..." the man murmurs. And, exhausted, he collapses sitting on the sloping sand, wrapping his arms around the legs of his son.

The creature remains standing; and as he understands his father's pain, he slowly caresses his head:

"Poor dad."

"It's getting late. It is going to be three o'clock. We should head back." said the father.

Together now, father and son undertake the return to the house.

"How did you not look at the sun to know the time ...?" The father murmurs still.

"I noticed, papa ... But when I was going to return, I saw Juan's herons, and I followed them ..."

"What you put me through, little one!"

"Dad ..." the boy also murmurs.

After a long silence:

"And the herons, did you kill them?" Asks the father.

"No."

Insignificant detail, after all. Under the red-hot sky and air, the man returns home with his son, on whose shoulders, almost as high as his own, the happy arms of his father swing forcefully. He returns drenched in sweat, and though broken in body and soul, he smiles with happiness.

He smiles in delighted happiness, since the father goes alone.

He has found no one, and his arm rests in the void. Because behind him, at the foot of a post and with his legs up, tangled in the barbed wire, his beloved son lies in the sun, dead since ten in the morning.

The Flies

While hiking on the mountain, several men cut down a tree the previous year. Its trunk now lay in its entirety, flattened against the ground. While the other trees have lost a large part of their bark during the fire, the tree keeps its bark almost intact. Hardly a charred strip along its entire length signals that there was a fire.

This event occurred last winter. Four months have passed. Amid the drought, the stunted tree always lies in a wasteland of ash. Sitting against the trunk, I am also still. Somewhere on my back, I have a spinal fracture. I fell after unluckily tripping against a stump. Just as I fell, I remained seated against the tree.

For a moment, I felt a fixed buzzing—the buzzing of the spinal cord injury in which my breath seems to flow. I can no longer move my hands and can barely feel the ashes with my fingers.

From this very moment, I acquire the certainty that my life will end soon.

Never has a more profound truth presented to my mind. All the other truths float, dance, like a very distant reverberation of another self. The only perception of my existence, but flagrant as a significant blow struck in silence, is that in a moment, I will die.

But when? How many seconds do I have left in which this exasperated living consciousness will give way to a calm corpse?

Nobody approaches this grazing: no mountain peak leads to it from any property. But, for the man sitting there, as for the trunk that supports him, the rains will come, as usual, wetting bark and clothing, and the suns will dry lichens and hair until the mountain regrows and unifies trees and skin, bones and shoe leather.

And there's nothing, nothing in the serenity of the environment that denounces such an event! Instead, through the trunks and black sections of the brush, from here or there, whatever the observation point, anyone can contemplate with perfect clarity the man whose life is about to end. So small is its place in the grazing and so clear the situation: the man is dying.

What is the truth worth in the face of the barbarous restlessness of the precise moment in which this resistance of life and this tremendous psychological torture will explode like a rocket, leaving as residue a corpse with his face fixed forever forward?

The buzzing grows louder and louder. A veil of dense darkness now closes over my eyes in which green rhombuses stand out. And immediately I see the walled door of a Moroccan souk, through one of whose leaves a herd of white colts escapes, while through the other a group of beheaded men comes running.

I want to close my eyes, and I can't do it anymore. I now see a small hospital room where four doctors try to convince me that I will not die. I watch them in silence, and they laugh as they follow my thoughts.

"Therefore," says one of them, "there's no more proof than the cage of flies. I have one."

"Flies?…"

"Yes," he says, "tracking green flies. You are not unaware that green flies sniff out the decay of meat long before the subject's death. The patient is still alive; they come, certain of their prey. They fly over the patient without hurry since they have already smelled death. It is the most effective means of forecasting death known. That is why I have some green flies, which I rent at a reasonable price. Where they enter, death will come soon. I can put them in the corridor when you are alone and open the door of the little cage, which, by the way, is a small coffin. You have no other task than to peer into the keyhole. If a fly comes in and you hear it buzzing, be sure the others will find their way to you too. I rent them at a reasonable price."

"Hospital…?" Suddenly the whitewashed room, the medicine cabinet, the doctors, and laughter disappear into a hum.

And abruptly, too, I see the revelation. It's the flies!

They are the ones that buzz. Since I have fallen, they have come without delay. Drowsy in the bush by the field, the flies have known about a safe prey in the vicinity. They have already smelled the decomposition of the seated man, by a process unknown to us, perhaps on the exhalation through the flesh of the severed spinal cord. Nevertheless, they came without delay and fluttered around without haste, measuring with their eyes the proportions of the nest that luck has just provided for their eggs.

But behold, this desperate desire to resist subsides and gives way to a blissful imponderability. I no longer feel like a fixed point on earth, rooted to it by severe torture. Instead, I think that the lightness of the ambient mist, the sunlight, the fecundity of the hour flows from me like life itself. I can go here, there, to this tree, to that vine, free of space and time. I can see, already far away, like a memory of isolated existence, I can still see a doll with unblinking eyes, a glassy-looking scarecrow, and rigid legs at the foot of a log. From the bosom of this expansion, I can get up and fly, fly.

And I fly, I fly with my companions around the fallen log, in the rays of the sun that lend their fire to our work of vital renewal.

About the Author

Horacio Quiroga, born in 1878, was a prolific Uruguayan poet and short story writer. He wrote eight books containing over 100 short stories in total.

Horacio's personal life was very chaotic. His father's death at the age of two and the suicide of his stepfather marked his childhood. When he came of age, he bought a small piece of land with his inheritance and married a beautiful young bride who inspired two of his most important works.

Living in the jungle with his wife and two children, Horacio published his most famous short story book: Jungle Tales. After moving to Buenos Aires in 1917, Quiroga lived in a basement with his children as he worked on the stories that would later be collected in several books, the first being "Historias de Amor, Locura y Muerte," or "Tales of Love, Madness, and Death," published in that same year.

Horacio Quiroga committed suicide on February 19, 1937.

www.ingramcontent.com/pod-product-compliance
Lightning Source LLC
Chambersburg PA
CBHW072112150726
47999CB00005B/2007